Penguin Science Fiction
Into Deepest Space

Sir Fred Hoyle, F.R.S., the well-known astronomer, writer, broadcaster, and television personality, is a Fellow of St John's College, Cambridge. He was Plumian Professor of Astronomy and Experimental Philosophy (1958–73) and Director of the Cambridge Institute of Theoretical Astronomy, which he founded (1961–73). In 1968 he was awarded the Gold Medal of the Royal Astronomical Society, becoming President in 1971. In 1968 he also received the Kalinga Prize given by the United Nations for promoting scientific understanding to a general audience. In 1969 he was elected an associate member of the American National Academy of Science – the highest U.S. honour for non-American scientists. He was knighted in 1972, and in 1974 was awarded a Royal Medal by Her Majesty the Queen in recognition of his distinguished contributions to theoretical physics and cosmology.

His other publications include *The Nature of the Universe* (1950; a Pelican), *Frontiers of Astronomy* (1956) and *Man in the Universe* (1966). His other novels include *The Black Cloud* (1957) and *October the First is Too Late* (1966). *Fifth Planet* (1963), *Rockets in Ursa Major* (1969), *Seven Steps to the Sun* (1970), *The Molecule Men* (1971), and *The Inferno* (1972) were written with his son, Geoffrey Hoyle. Fred Hoyle has also published a play, *Rockets in Ursa Major* (1962), and is the joint author of *A for Andromeda* (1962), a television serial.

Geoffrey Hoyle was born in 1942 and is Fred Hoyle's son. Educated at Bryanston School in Dorset and Cambridge University, he worked in the field of modern communications and motion pictures before becoming a full-time writer. Currently he and his wife, Valerie, are busy creating a new home in a Lancashire farm-house, watched over closely by their old Pyrenean mountain dog. They both love travelling abroad and swimming in warm water, but these come second to Geoffrey's pistol shooting. In this exacting sport he is recognized as one of the leading marksmen in the country.

Fred Hoyle
and Geoffrey Hoyle

Into Deepest
Space

edited by Barbara Hoyle

Penguin Books

Penguin Books Ltd, Harmondsworth,
Middlesex, England
Penguin Books, 625 Madison Avenue,
New York, New York 10022, U.S.A.
Penguin Books Australia Ltd, Ringwood,
Victoria, Australia
Penguin Books Canada Ltd, 2801 John Street,
Markham, Ontario, Canada L3R 1B4
Penguin Books (N.Z.) Ltd, 182–190 Wairau Road,
Auckland 10, New Zealand

First published in Great Britain by Heinemann 1975
Published in Penguin Books 1977

Copyright © Fred Hoyle and Geoffrey Hoyle, 1974
All rights reserved

Made and printed in Great Britain by
Hazell Watson & Viney Ltd, Aylesbury, Bucks
Set in Linotype Baskerville

Except in the United States of America,
this book is sold subject to the condition that
it shall not, by way of trade or otherwise, be lent,
re-sold, hired out, or otherwise circulated without
the publisher's prior consent in any form of
binding or cover other than that in which it is
published and without a similar condition
including this condition being imposed on the
subsequent purchaser

Prologue

We all made our way out of the rain and into the building. Betelgeuse was being questioned about the evasive action he'd taken over the ground-to-air missiles. His replies were short and curt. I felt as he must. Anxious. Wanting news of what had happened out there in space.

'It won't be long now,' Alcyone said, coming over.

Drinks began to appear. It struck me as rather funny. Were they celebrating our safe return, or the fantastic destruction we had wrought?

'There's a message from your ship,' said Ganges to Betelgeuse, handing him a micro-earpiece. A message was given. His face didn't alter but I thought I noticed a slight glint in his eye.

'Gentlemen,' said Betelgeuse. 'My second-in-command has signalled to say the enemy has retreated with very heavy losses.'

A cheer of relief went up, and even Betelgeuse looked reasonably happy. There were handshakes and a raising of glasses.

I made my way over to Betelgeuse. 'I suppose you'll be on your way,' I said.

'Hm. I'm not sure about that,' he said. I realized that his smile was a front.

'What's wrong?'

'This,' he said, giving me the micro-earpiece.

'For the time being you have won. But I am not defeated so easily.' The message came across in English. I listened to it for several moments. It just repeated itself. Betelgeuse took the micro-earpiece out of my hand.

'Smile,' he said. I did, as we turned to the rest of the party, who nodded smilingly back, unknowing and innocent of things to come.

1 Borrowed Time

I sat at my desk and flicked the last pages of my diary closed. It was now almost three years since I'd returned from the successful mission with Betelgeuse, when he and I had dropped a lithium bomb into the Sun to ward off an attack by the Yela. The lithium bomb produced such a fantastic solar outburst that not only did the Yela space-ships fry, but even to this day the solar system was being bombarded with lethal high-energy particles.

What none of us had realized at the time was that the space around the Earth would be totally uninhabitable for so long. Even Betelgeuse, the Earth's ally from Ursa Major, was becoming despondent about ever being able to rejoin his fleet of ships, which was still parked somewhere deep in space outside the solar system. Appallingly de-pressing to him was the lack of communication with his own people, since all radio signals in the solar system were now being absorbed by a flood of electrons in inter-planetary space.

The first flush of success from our mission had, of course, been deeply satisfying. I was awarded my present physics post at World Space Headquarters. Betelgeuse and his second-in-command, the ubiquitous Rigel, were given the go-ahead by W.S.HQ. to develop and produce a new breed of ION nuclear engines. These new engines were to power not only existing ships but a whole new generation of ships that were being constructed to Betelgeuse's specifi-cations.

While he and Rigel were thus busy with their develop-ment and construction program, I had spent much of the

7

three years training as an astronaut. Obviously I couldn't go out to any of the space labs, because of the complete halt in space travel. Instead I busied myself catching up on new developments in physics, but it was a desultory effort. By now, people had forgotten about the Yela and were beginning to resent being Earthbound. There was a lot of grumbling that I was the man who stopped space travel – which, in a way, was true. Even a close friend, Colonel Rhodes, had been distinctly cool on my last visit to London.

The only person who didn't seem to change was Alcyone. She was one of Betelgeuse's crew. After the lithium bomb affair she had accepted a job as my assistant at W.S.H.Q. Whatever seemed wrong with the world, or with my colleagues, she never faltered. She was always there by my side helping and encouraging me.

'What is it?' she asked, bringing me back to reality with a bump.

'I'm becoming morbid. My mind has become cluttered with trivialities. I can't think.'

'Perhaps you would be better off back in England.'

'Self-pity, that's what is really wrong with me,' I said with an attempted grin. 'Now you mention it, England seems almost in another time and place. No, I don't think I would find peace of mind there.'

We strolled arm in arm from the characterless concrete building. A short walk brought us to the top of a small cliff. There stretching out before us rolled the deep blue of the Pacific.

The old sites at Cape Kennedy and then at Houston had long ago become politically unacceptable and had been replaced perforce by the present spot in Baja California. The area around Sebastian Vizcarrio Bay became the new World Space Headquarters. Here, among the cactus and the sagebrush, vast areas of concrete, glass and tarmac grew up. The base itself was designed to cater to tens of thousands of spacecraft, while a veritable city, situated a little inland from the space station, had been built to house the flight crews and technicians from the centre.

Alcyone and I were lucky in our allocation of an apartment, which had been done by random-number selection. The superb view of the mountains from our quarters helped us to forget the hot arid plain of the launch pads only a few kilometres away.

'You are required on the telephone,' a disembodied voice announced, breaking into the silence.

'Hm?'

'You're wanted on the telephone, Dr Warboys.'

For a moment I'd forgotten the find-you-anywhere bleep attached to my overalls.

'Come on,' said Alcyone, giving me a push towards the science block.

I hurried into a small booth near the main entrance and pressed a button on the vision phone.

'Ah, Dick,' said Dr John Newman, as his face appeared on the screen, 'could you drop in to see me for a moment?'

'Certainly,' I grunted. Newman's image, distorted and elongated by a fault in the phone system, disappeared as he switched the circuit off.

'Newman has something on his mind,' I said, rejoining Alcyone.

We looked at each other for a long moment.

'Better go and hear what he has to say,' Alcyone said at last.

Newman might be wondering why I hadn't turned in some brilliant new piece of research work. The majority of scientists on the base seemed to turn in scientific papers with a fair amount of regularity. But then it might be something else, something I'd been fearing, half-expecting. I knocked on the door to the Chief Administrator's super-carpeted office. It slid open.

'Come in,' Newman said, 'take a chair. I thought you might be interested in these,' he went on, handing me a folder. Inside was a set of astronomical spectra, obviously of the Balmer series of hydrogen. Nothing struck me as odd, until on the last spectrum I could see that the lines were all systematically displaced from where they would normally have been. Then a closer look at the earlier spectra showed that the hydrogen gas was being steadily accelerated.

'Quite a lot of hydrogen appears to be accelerating towards us,' I said at length.

'Correct. Those plates were taken some weeks ago.'

'Where is the stuff located?' I asked.

'Those prints have just come in from Malcolm Jones at the Tucson Observatory.'

'Hydrogen!'

'Yes, hydrogen,' grunted Newman. 'I remember Betelgeuse telling me that the Yela could move vast quantities of hydrogen around the galaxy.'

'Why wasn't this noticed before?'

'I suggest you go straight over to Tucson and find out. Check all their records. There's no point in taking any chances, especially when the Yela might be involved.'

My mind seemed to be clearing rapidly. 'Do they have any idea of the quantity involved?'

'Dick, pack a bag and get yourself to Tucson. That's for you to find out.'

'It could mean a defence alert.'

'That's exactly what *I* have to find out,' snapped Newman conclusively.

I sped back to my office.

'What happened?' asked Alcyone, brightly, as usual.

'Some hydrogen has been found, apparently quite close to our solar system.'

'Hydrogen,' said Alcyone slowly, the expression of confidence fading from her face.

'I have to go to Tucson. Do you want to come?'

'No, you go. I must send a message to Betelgeuse.'

'I don't know whether the Yela is behind it. It could all be a false alarm.'

10

'Maybe, but Betelgeuse will want to know.'

'I shouldn't be in Tucson long. It really depends on how complete their records are.'

The VTOL stood on the launch pad shimmering in the brilliant sunlight. It struck me as I stepped aboard that I could have dealt with the investigation just as easily from my own office. However, I was glad of the chance to escape for a brief moment from the general feeling of depression on the base.

Over the years at W.S.HQ. I had learnt enough of flying and navigation to have developed an uncomfortable fear of flying with other pilots. The outer door of the VTOL clicked shut. There was a moment's pause, then the chemical engines ignited. A few seconds later the sickness I felt in the pit of my stomach was replaced by the steady g force building up as the plane accelerated.

Thirty minutes later the VTOL was hovering over the University of Arizona's landing pad. Another five minutes and I was greeted by Malcolm Jones, head of the astronomy department at the University. He was dressed in a white shirt, red shorts and the usual western string tie.

'How's Baja California?'

'Hot and dusty. Well, Malcolm, what's all this I hear about a wagon train of hydrogen moving into the solar system?'

'Looks like one of these runaway interstellar clouds. Except that the column density is very high.'

I digested this remark as we raced along the monorail to Jones's office.

'What d'you mean quantitatively by very high?' I asked, once we were seated.

'Well, take a look at these.' Jones handed me a series of computer printouts. 'They cover the period from June 2010 to June this year,' he added.

'When were the pictures you sent John Newman taken?'

'Between the twenty-third and thirtieth of August.'

'Two weeks ago,' I murmured, as I ran my eye down the column of figures in front of me. Slowly the situation clarified. Since June 2010 there had been a steady increase in the quantity of hydrogen just outside the solar system.

'This is quite staggering,' I said at length.

'What?'

'These figures on the quantity of hydrogen. If I'm interpreting all this correctly, it must amount to something like 10^{15} tons.'

'Yes, something like that. Astonishingly, ten years ago there was scarcely a trace of hydrogen in that direction.' This was exceedingly unpalatable information.

'How did you come by these?' I asked, indicating the sheets in front of me.

'A Ph.D. student working on the chemical nature of the interstellar medium. He wanted all relevant information on the quantity of hydrogen in space around the solar system. Most students would have assumed there was little or none, but not young Bob Sentinel. He was out to find something unusual and he did.'

'Is this hydrogen moving?'

'It would appear to be.'

'In what direction?'

'Inwards. Towards the Sun. Towards us. And pretty fast at that.'

'How fast?'

'I did some calculations before you arrived,' Jones replied. 'It seems we shall be immersed in this hydrogen within a matter of months – at most. Sooner than that, if it goes on accelerating.'

This confirmed my worst fears. 'May I have a copy of these printouts?'

'Take 'em,' said Jones, watching my reactions. 'It seems I'm missing something,' he added.

I shook my head. 'Betelgeuse was right. The Yela is of a higher intellectual order than I gave it credit for.'

'Which means?'

'I never believed anyone could move vast quantities of hydrogen around space, as we do in the laboratory.'

'Sorry, I don't understand.'

'The Yela can destroy the Earth by wrapping a blanket of hydrogen around our atmosphere. Then all it needs do to destroy us is just to press a little of the hydrogen into the atmosphere itself. The hydrogen and the oxygen in our atmosphere combine together with an immense release of heat. The generation of heat causes the gas to rise and more hydrogen is sucked down. Within seconds the whole atmosphere is a raging inferno.'

'What a way to go.'

'For the moment I'd appreciate it if you could keep this to yourself.'

'Of course,' murmured Jones deep in thought.

He was still sunk within himself when an hour later, having collected all the data I needed, I took my leave. The VTOL was no longer on the landing pad. Without hesitation I phoned for a taxi. The excitement inside my brain mounted steadily as I waited. By the time the taxi had landed on the pad in front of me, I'd forgotten where I wanted to go. A moment of deliberation and consultation with the driver revealed that I'd intended to go to the airport. On the way I attempted to bribe the driver to take me all the way to W.S.HQ., but he wasn't an adventurous man and declined the fare.

I began to sharpen my wits against the problem of how the Yela had managed to collect such a quantity of hydrogen and funnel it towards the solar system. Betelgeuse had told me a lot about the effects of an atmosphere burning off but little concerning the transportation of hydrogen.

'We're at the terminal,' drawled a voice in my ear.

'What?'

'Airport.'

'Oh, thank you,' I said, handing the man my credit card. He laboriously punched the information from the credit card onto his mini-computer. Seconds later a receipt was issued and I was on my way across the airport to hire myself a plane.

'Can I be of help?' said a polite voice from behind the Hertz desk.

'Hm.' I stared at the girl dressed in canary yellow. 'Yes, I'd like to hire a plane.'

'Certainly, sir,' she said, handing me a card that listed the different types of aircraft I could hire.

'I'll have the quickest one you have,' I replied, without looking at her card.

'Your licence, please,' she said, starting to type out the necessary data for the firm's computer. An absurd thought crossed my mind. What would happen if one's data got lost in the complicated cross-computerization that makes up today's communication system? Here was this pretty girl busy finding out from a dozen computers whether I was who I said I was. Whether I was in credit. Was my licence valid. Who were my parents. Did I suffer from mental illness. The list could go on forever. Betelgeuse, Rigel and Alcyone had never been subjected to cross-computerization. They used a computer to keep themselves alive in their spacecraft, not for tabulating endless statistics.

'Your Apache 3CF will be at Door 5 in ten minutes,' said the girl, handing me a bundle of punched cards, which told me that I was who I thought I was – at least for today.

'Thanks.'

'You're welcome. Have a pleasant trip.'

A row of public phone booths caught my eye. It took W.S.H.Q. quite a while to locate Alcyone, which I found intolerable.

'Hello, Dick,' she said at last, her smiling face appearing on the screen in front of me.

'I'm on my way. Could you find out where Betelgeuse is and let him know that something urgent has cropped up?'

'Is it bad?'

'I'll tell you when I get back. Oh, and could you let Newman know I'm returning? See you soon.' I pressed the cancellation button and Alcyone's face faded from the screen.

My mind turned back to the problem of the Yela, but without significant effect. If the Yela couldn't be stopped, we were finished. It was as simple as that.

I followed a passage down to Door 5, where the small four-seater jet was parked.

'Your cards, please,' said a voice from behind me.

'Hm,' I murmured and turned to be confronted by another girl dressed in canary yellow. I handed over my deck, which she examined and then handed back. I hurried across the tarmac to where a man in canary yellow overalls was standing.

'Good morning, sir. Have you flown one before, sir?'

'Yes, thank you.'

'Have a good trip then,' he said, stepping out from the pilot's door.

I thanked him again and climbed into the narrow seat. On the radio computer I typed out all the relevant details of the aircraft, of myself and of my destination. Then I waited while a gigantic air-traffic control computer somewhere in California sifted through the information. When it had found a clear route, a green light flashed in front of me. I fired up the engines and taxied to the end of the runway. Again I waited. After the computer had checked my flight plan yet again, the throttles of the plane were released by the computer.

As a pilot I have a great desire to get on with the job. When the throttles were released I opened them into full power. With the engines screaming at this abuse, I released the brakes.

Now I had to concentrate on getting into the air. I watched the air-speed indicator rise slowly, and at the same time attempted to keep the plane on a straight and even keel. As the air-speed indicator reached takeoff velocity, I crossed my fingers and slowly eased the plane off the ground. Once airborne my worries were over, since the automatic pilot then took over control. I inched around on my seat until I was relatively comfortable. Disconnected thoughts tumbled through my brain. Over the past three years the edge of my own mental alertness had been worn down by an inability to see things clearly. The success and publicity I'd received had somehow blunted my capabilities. A horrifying reality: success brings complacency, or at least it did with me. I should have let Betelgeuse take the credit and retired back to my personal research.

But this large quantity of hydrogen floating around where it shouldn't have been was beginning to sharpen my wits. My eye moved over the columns of figures that Malcolm Jones had given to me. The meaning of these numbers filtered back into my consciousness, releasing emotions that slowly turned to anger. It was the same cold anger that had spurred my mind into conceiving the idea of the lithium bomb.

The nose of the plane dipped and started its approach to the landing strip at W.S.HQ. The day was crystal clear, with the shimmering yellows and reds of the arid country to my left and the deep blue of the Pacific to my right.

Suddenly the plane was hurled from its course by terrific turbulence. The automatic pilot seemed about as ready as I was for the emergency. The plane spiralled Earthwards. I fought the flying printout sheets from my face. Through the giddiness I was beginning to feel, I managed to turn the automatic pilot off and start to correct the furious descent.

Since my knowledge of aerobatics was extremely limited, it was as well that I had recently been training under extreme g forces.

The small plane whipped downward for several seconds before I could level it out. The yellows and reds of the desert suddenly became lumps of rock, deep canyons and hills. The next moment the nose of the plane came up, as specks of foam from the Pacific breakers sprayed onto the windscreen. I opened the throttle and quickly regained height.

I sat for a moment covered from head to toe in paper. I'd never come across turbulence like that before. At last it dawned on me that the turbulence must have been produced by another aircraft.

I switched the automatic pilot back on and collected the sadly torn and crumpled printout sheets. The plane completed a circuit of the landing area and started its approach once more. The computer seemed totally unaware of my shattered physical state. I'd very nearly been sucked to my death by some raving lunatic.

Under normal circumstances I would have left the delicate matter of landing to the plane's computer, but this time the computer had goofed, so I switched the automatic pilot off and took command of the situation myself. To my surprise and pleasure there was but a gentle bump and I was down. Gradual pressure on the brakes and an easing of the throttles brought the plane to a stop about halfway down the runway. I taxied the plane to the parking area. As I dropped to the ground, a canary car raced across the tarmac.

'Gee, we thought you'd bought it,' said the breathless hire-company representative.

'What the devil was it?' I asked, handing the man the aircraft documents.

'An intercontinental rocket, I believe. Came in like a bat out of hell.'

'Civilian or military?'

'I don't think it was civilian. Leastways it didn't land here.'

'Thanks. I hope the computer wasn't too upset,' I said and started towards the exit. Once outside I stepped onto a moving roadway. Within a few minutes I was at W.S.H Q.

Alcyone was not at her desk or in my office. A moment's flash of disappointment and then I was down to a detailed study of the mass of jumbled papers before me.

'Reporting for duty,' boomed a familiar voice.

I turned to see Betelgeuse and Alcyone standing in the doorway both looking like the Cheshire Cat. Betelgeuse was wearing one of his orange-red sweaters, and was attempting to smoke a cigar of enormous proportions. After getting through perhaps an inch of one of them he would usually fling it away, shouting 'disgusting taste'.

'Sorry about the turbulence,' he roared, clapping me on the back.

'You nearly killed me.'

'Nonsense. I have great faith in your ability as a pilot,' he chuckled.

'You'd better take a look at this,' I said, prodding the pile of paper in front of me.

In a flash the genial expression on Betelgeuse's face was gone, to be replaced by a look of grim foreboding. Without speaking we began, all three of us, to examine columns of figures, figures that sounded the death knell of our species. The Yela had made good its threat.

2 Two Steps to Doomsday

We worked at the computer printouts until early the following morning.

'Well?' I asked, as Betelgeuse sat back in his chair and mopped his brow.

'It would appear that the Yela is working true to form. A large mass of hydrogen is already within the solar system. It appears to be headed directly towards the Earth. If it maintains its present speed, it will reach the Earth not many weeks from now.'

'What I'd like to know is how the devil the Yela does it,' I mused.

'Dick, this planet is about to be destroyed and all you can think of is how the thing was done. I've actually seen planets burn, but the mechanics of it all are still a mystery.'

'I don't expect you to know the answer. All I'm saying is that you, the Yela, and others on millions of planets throughout the Universe have intelligences greater than mine. So I'm just trying to catch up a bit. You are able to travel deep into space. To me that is fantastic. Now I want to know how the Yela moves 10^{15} tons of hydrogen around. It doesn't do it with tankers.'

'You have made your point, and if we are still here next year we'll delve into the engineering problem,' said Betelgeuse in his curious accent. If it weren't for the accent his English would by now have been perfect.

'We must inform the authorities of what we suspect and evacuate as many people as possible,' he added.

'Where are all the refugees to go?'

'They will do as we have done,' replied Betelgeuse, 'wander the galaxy until they find another habitable planet.'

'I don't like it. I don't want to leave the Earth. In any case won't the Yela just systematically destroy all our ships?'

'Well, that won't affect you then, will it?' Betelgeuse said with a grimace.

I ignored him, and continued, 'I would calculate . . .'

Both Alcyone and Betelgeuse began to laugh at my stubborn persistence. Then we realized that John Newman was standing there in the corridor outside the office. To his greeting we answered, 'Good morning!' in unison, all trying to be serious again. This was hard for Alcyone because by nature she was always laughing and gay.

'From your cheerfulness, can I assume the Yela threat to be unfounded?' Newman asked.

'To the contrary,' replied Betelgeuse, 'there is a high volume of hydrogen moving toward this planet at great speed.'

'Why wasn't I told of this before?'

'We have only just finished analysing the information I brought back from Tucson. I would suggest that world governments be immediately informed of the present situation. In the meantime we shall attempt to confirm our findings.'

'Why should the end of our world be funny?' asked Newman, apparently transfixed in what looked like a steady state of shock.

Alcyone after a prolonged silence took hold of the man's arm and gently led him from the office.

'We're all beginning to crack,' I said, wiping sweat from my face.

At length I asked, 'I suppose the radio absorption is still hampering communications with the ships of your fleet?'

'Afraid so,' grunted Betelgeuse disconsolately. He had

been a long time without news of his deep-space companions.

'It might be worth having a round-the-clock listen just in case something can be picked up.'

'That is being done already. But there is only static.'

'It's not a pleasant thought, but could the Yela have got to them?'

'I have been hoping the Yela is too preoccupied moving the hydrogen around to worry about our ships. But I think I will make another check on the situation.'

While Betelgeuse went off to make his inquiries, Alcyone and I set about writing a report on our findings. In principle, of course, it was hard to prove that the hydrogen was for burning up the Earth. It might have been a freak astronomical occurrence, unlikely but possible. Only continuing observation of the situation would finally resolve the question, but by then it would probably be too late to take effective action. Clearly it was important to send up an unmanned probe, to see what was happening above the Earth's atmosphere. I felt there might be a good chance of launching and returning such a probe before the situation deteriorated. I cursed the fact that all Earth-to-space communications were jammed. Otherwise it would certainly have been possible to activate some of the orbiting laboratory equipment.

'Shall I send this to the representatives?' asked Alcyone, holding up the report.

'Better send it through Newman. He won't pigeonhole it.'

'No, but he might dither. He didn't look too stable just now.'

'On the verge of breakdown, I'd say.'

'You still want it to go through Newman?'

'Oh, God knows. Send it to the representatives and have done with it. But give a copy of it to Newman.'

'What will they do?'

'Oh, some will report immediately to their governments. Others will await further information, and get themselves clobbered from here to the Moon for not reporting when the others do. Then sealed envelopes specially prepared for the occasion will be opened. Inside them will be the names of important persons who have been allocated places in the spaceships.'

'Do they understand the consequences?'

'I don't think the chosen few will realize the dangers involved in their escape. If they survive the radiation in the Earth's magnetosphere, there'll still be the Yela to deal with.'

'The risk of radiation poisoning must surely be generally known,' Alcyone said.

'I think people realize the risk, in a general sort of way, but not the full magnitude of it. Nor the full magnitude of what is likely to be involved in the long run. You know, all the spaceships that have been built during the last few years have been built to military specifications. All your ships were built to accommodate people for long durations in space.'

'Of course. Otherwise we would never have survived in space.'

'Our governments have simply built themselves a more efficient fighting fleet, not a fleet equipped at all for deep-space travel.'

'So whoever travels in one of these Earth ships has only a poor chance of surviving. That is a big pity.'

'All the same, we'd better send the report off, straight-away,' I concluded.

Alcyone went quickly out of the office with a sheaf of papers, while I tidied up my desk and then walked slowly back to the apartment. It was chilly in the still desert air. The sun was just beginning to shine over the tops of the mountains. Would anyone in the years to come ever visit this planet and wonder at the charred black earth? With the atmosphere gone no winds would blow. A deathly silence would replace the voices of the millions who had once inhabited this still golden world.

But as I strolled along no sense of depression overcame me. I was still impelled by a strong desire to struggle on for as long as possible. And above all else I wanted to see how the hand was won or lost. I pushed the door of the apartment open, threw myself on the bed and fell into a deep sleep.

They say there is no rest for the wicked, and I was rudely awakened by a violent shaking.

'Come on, Dick, this is no time for sleeping,' I heard Betelgeuse's voice saying through the mists of sleep.

'Come on? Come on for what?' I mumbled furiously.

'Coffee.'

'What I've never been able to understand is how you people manage to remain fit and well on a couple of hours' cat-napping,' I said, taking the coffee cup.

'Years of training. When you've been looking over your shoulder for as long as I have, you'll cat-nap.'

Betelgeuse flung away a black cigar, almost a foot long, grunting as he always did, 'Disgusting taste! Look, Dick, I've been doing some updated calculations. The hydrogen cloud will be in the vicinity of the Earth's atmosphere in a dangerously short length of time, shorter than you realized. Whatever is decided here on Earth by the authorities is now their problem. I shall take off no later than noon tomorrow.'

'Wow! That's a bit soon, isn't it?'

'Not too soon for me. The hydrogen is acting to dry up the interplanetary electrons. There are indications that communication may become possible again.'

'With your fleet?'

'I think so. I may be able to get through to the others, once I get my ship out beyond Jupiter.'

'How about the local radiation, the stuff in our own magnetosphere?'

'I am dealing with the problem now. We'll just have

to rely on heavy suiting material for the extra protection.'

'Which might not be enough.'

'Remember, my ship is much better protected than your military ones, which everybody insisted on building against my advice.'

'It is the true nature of mankind, at least of the terrestrial variety, to learn from mistakes, not from example,' I pontificated. 'Has the new engine been fitted in the Earth ships?'

'Oh yes. Every ship is now equipped with one. Unfortunately the unit is smaller than I would have liked because of the need for chemical rockets. What, of course, is not known is whether they will be as reliable as our engines. Your engineers have made what they call improvements to our well-tried design.'

'Have there been any reactions yet from the public?' I asked.

'Not really. The news media still haven't pieced together the full story. I suppose they'll wait for confirmation of what is happening.'

'That wouldn't be very typical, would it?' I mused.

'The situation will be well known within hours. And what will you be doing yourself this time tomorrow?' Betelgeuse added.

'Sleeping, I should think.'

'Don't you have the will to survive?'

'Of course.'

'You realize that Alcyone will wish to rejoin her own people?'

'Yes, I know.'

'And you?' pressed Betelgeuse.

'To be frank, I just don't know whether I could really adjust to spending the remaining years of my life in a spaceship.'

'You're just as stubborn as those engineers I've been dealing with over the past years.'

'Didn't your own forefathers feel reluctant to relinquish what had been theirs for many thousands of years?'

'Unfortunately there is little recorded as to what the early generations of space families thought about their environment. I would reason that they were too involved with survival to worry much about it.'

'Let's see how today goes. Then I'll make up my mind.'

'Sometimes I wish we'd never come to this part of the galaxy.'

'At least I'm glad you came. Our technology needed a hefty kick in the right direction. Talking of superintellects, have you reasoned out yet how the Yela moved that gas around?'

'No, I haven't,' said Betelgeuse, a note of despair creeping into his voice.

'It puzzles me. It can't just gather up a cloud of gas and push it through space.'

'Maybe it can! While you are wasting time delving into the transport problems of moving gas clouds I'm going again to the radio centre to see if anything more is happening.'

'Fine. By the way, why did you come round and wake me up? Was it for my health?'

'I'd almost forgotten. I just wanted to say that there is always space on our ship for an extra person should you wish to come.'

For a moment we looked at each other and then he was gone.

Betelgeuse and I had developed over the years a friendship that weathered all the storms of our different personalities. Betelgeuse with his distant, detached, logical reactions; myself moody, temperamental, selfish, very sentimental and only under pressure able to generate ideas of any significance. While my curiosity was largely reserved for research in pure science, his main interest lay in the more practical side of engineering in its various forms.

Wandering around the galaxy might provide ample

time for the development of new ideas, but I knew I would dislike the claustrophobic atmosphere of a spaceship. If it meant my survival I would surely go, but if there were a chance of remaining on Earth I would stay.

I dialled my office number.

'Hello,' said Alcyone, as she appeared on the screen.

'Is there any new information on the hydrogen cloud?' I asked.

'It is definitely closing on the Earth.'

'How much confirmation from other sources is there?'

'This good enough?' said Alcyone, picking up an enormous pile of computer printouts.

'Yes,' I grinned wryly. 'Look, I'm just going to have a quick shower, then I'll be with you.'

'All right. See you soon,' said Alcyone and switched off.

Signs of intense new activity were already obvious. The miles of launching pads were already filled with the tall slender needle shapes of spacecraft. I could hear the hum of gigantic electric motors as they pumped rocket fuel into the ships from storage tanks deep inside the Earth. Even as I approached my office block I could feel the ground vibrating beneath my feet. The vast air strip to the left of the launch pads was already cluttered with intercontinental Pegasus IV's, while a motley collection of small jet planes had been left untidily around the edge of the strip.

'I've been in touch with most of the radio telescopes throughout the world and they all confirm that hydrogen is building up some hundred thousand miles above the atmosphere,' exclaimed Alcyone, as I strode into the office.

'Incredible. It's already happening. Much quicker than I thought it would.' I started hunting for a diagram of the solar system.

'The density is still rather low, though.'

'Still rather low,' I repeated. 'Better keep a close check on that.' Alcyone hesitated for a moment and then went off out of the office.

Young men with excited faces kept appearing with vast bundles of computer paper. Every time a new batch came in I carefully checked it to compare results. The hydrogen didn't appear to be coming any closer. Nor was it getting any more dense. I began to wonder whether the Yela had run out of steam. The amount of energy required to transport all this hydrogen across space must have been enormous.

'We're back on the air.' I heard Betelgeuse's excited voice in the outer office. 'Dick,' he roared, bursting through the door and throwing away another gargantuan cigar, 'we have communication with my fleet.' His red face almost matched the colour of his sweater.

'That's wonderful. Where are they?'

'Beyond Pluto. Keeping out of the way of the Yela.' A great grin of relief split his face.

'You say that the Yela never left the area of the solar system?'

'It remained just outside it. Somewhere in line with the plane of the galaxy as far as I can determine.'

'Where did the hydrogen come from?'

'Very simple,' said Betelgeuse obviously having saved this piece of news till last. 'It made it.'

'Seriously?'

'About a year after the lithium bomb exploded, several ships from our fleet went off on scout duty, to see what the Yela were doing. They found large quantities of hydrogen being *produced*. Since all radio communication was out of action, they tried to send a ship down here to warn the Earth, but unfortunately the local radiation levels were too high and too dangerous.'

'Dr Warboys,' said a young man, poking his head round the office door.

'Yes.'

'This is for you, sir,' he said, and pushed a large wire trolley full of printouts into the middle of the room.

'Thanks.'

The lad smiled and left.

'You wanted a close check, didn't you?' said Alcyone, popping her head around the door.

'Sure I did,' I agreed, feeling that I'd lost a point in the game somewhere. I picked up the top sheets and started reading. 'Hey, look at this,' I exclaimed. Betelgeuse came and peered at the figures I was tapping with my finger.

'There is an actual decrease in the density of hydrogen. Look!'

'Here,' said Alcyone, holding out another sheet.

'The blasted stuff is evaporating!' I shouted in amazed excitement. 'I believe it's evaporating. The damned stuff is evaporating!'

'Why should it evaporate?' asked Betelgeuse, pulling more paper from the basket.

'I suppose because the streams of particles from the Sun are heating it up. The Sun is pushing it out, away from the solar system.'

'The excess of particles brought about by the lithium-bomb explosion?' asked Alcyone.

'I would think so.'

'Yet the Yela must have thought about the Sun,' said Betelgeuse with a frown. 'The Yela does not usually make such mistakes.' Betelgeuse continued to look very thoughtful.

'Hang on to these,' I said, passing a bundle of papers to Alcyone.

'Where are you off to now?'

'To see Newman,' I said and left. In my absence I hoped that Betelgeuse would voice some of his inner thoughts to Alcyone. If he decided to retire into deep space with his fleet, I could hardly blame him. Yet his superb technology was too valuable for the Earth to lose. I hoped Alcyone might persuade him and all his people to stay now that the latest threat from the Yela seemed as if it must come to naught – thanks once again to the Sun.

As I approached Newman's office, I saw a large crowd.

Judging by the equipment they had about them, I guessed they were the V.I.P.s bound for interstellar travel. I eased my way carefully through them until I was confronted by two very large policemen.

'I would like a word with Dr Newman,' I whispered to the one on the left, the one with the broken nose. 'It's on official business,' I added, taking my W.S.H.Q. security pass from my pocket. The M.P. grabbed hold of it and scrutinized it. Then he passed it over to his companion, who peered at it in the same suspicious manner.

'Just a minute,' said the broken-nosed fellow, walking off into the distance. It was twenty minutes before he was back. Returning my pass, he jerked a thumb in the direction of Newman's office, adding a succinct, 'O.K., bud.'

Inside the office it was even more chaotic than outside. I noticed through swaying bodies John Newman sitting to one side of his desk, staring straight into space. As I pushed and shoved, some of the faces I passed suddenly looked very familiar. I stopped and stared. Here were virtually all the heads of governments from all over the world.

'What is it?' Newman asked when at last I reached him.

'Is there anywhere we could have . . .'

'A quiet word? As you see, not a hope.'

'I just wanted to tell you that it appears that the hydrogen is evaporating and that the Yela is nowhere to be seen.' Although there was an intense hubbub, my remark must somehow have been heard. The uproar died as if an electronic switch had been pressed. Within a second you could have heard a whisper. I glanced around the room from world leader to world leader. As I did so, I wondered just how I was going to explain the report I had issued so confidently only a few hours before.

3 World in Crisis

John Newman looked at me with a blank expression, as though he'd not heard what I'd said.

'Say that again, brother,' bellowed a swarthy fellow standing close by.

'The hydrogen,' I repeated, 'has been, or is, evaporating.'

'Is what?' chimed in an English voice.

'Evaporating,' I said a little more firmly.

Snippets of conversation broke out everywhere through the room.

'How can hydrogen evaporate?'

'Hell, I've been dragged to this goddamned place just to be told there's nothing happening.'

'Whoever started this hoax will soon find he isn't the only one with a sense of humour,' continued the English voice.

Newman scowled in my direction. He would take no responsibility for the situation. It was my head that was in the noose.

'Have you got a copy of my report?' I asked.

Newman nodded toward the desk.

'What sort of joke is this?' asked a heavy voice close by my ear.

'Gentlemen, may I have your attention, please?' I said as soon as I was safely situated on the far side of the desk.

'Bloody scientists. Always jumping up and down like a bunch of bloody jack rabbits,' interrupted a big heavy-set man with an Australian accent.

'Gentlemen. Before we get to explanations I would refer

you to paragraph nine of the report. It states very simply that before further conclusions can be reached, a detailed study of the hydrogen will be necessary. It goes on to say that all governments will be notified as to the seriousness of the situation once details are known.'

'So what?' bawled the swarthy fellow.

'It would appear that you all thought the situation serious enough to come here. I assume you did your own checking on the situation and I presume you intended to be the first to get away from the Earth.' By now my voice had a backlash edge in it, for I had suddenly decided to take no more nonsense. At the back of my mind now was the thought of Betelgeuse and his ship, taking off from the Earth within a few hours. I could see that I might be on that ship after all.

'Damned upstart,' exclaimed the swarthy fellow, puffing out his cheeks.

'Stuff it,' I rapped back, as I glowered at the sea of faces in front of me.

'You are in no position to criticize us,' said a slender individual with an Italian accent.

'I shall now tell you what is known concerning the hydrogen that has appeared in our solar system,' I went on in as level a voice as I could manage.

The murmur of voices rose angrily at this statement.

'Gentlemen, gentlemen,' shouted someone above the din, 'let us hear what the man has to say. It appears that the present danger has passed. But we might very well have to decide on a future policy, to ensure that the present situation remains the same.'

'First sensible thing you've said today, Ivan,' remarked an American general. 'What's your name, sir?'

'Warboys. Richard Warboys,' I replied.

'Oh, I know you,' said an English officer with braid protruding from his ears, 'you're the fellow who threw the lithium bomb at the Sun.'

I nodded and the whole room erupted in conversation.

'Would it be too much to request a chair?' an elderly Frenchman asked.

'Hang on a minute,' said Newman, turning to me.

I waited deep in thought while several chairs were brought into the room.

'Gentlemen,' I said at length, 'it would appear from a preliminary investigation of all the known information that hydrogen was present in vast quantities near the Earth. The intervention of nature, however, has evaporated the hydrogen before it could be used as a weapon to destroy the Earth. Even so, it is very important that in our moment of jubilation we do not overlook the Yela's power. The Yela is a creature of superior technological knowledge, and must therefore not be underestimated.'

'Where did the hydrogen come from?' asked an Oriental gentleman from the left side of the room.

'The hydrogen is thought to have been somewhere outside the solar system and then pushed towards the earth.'

'Of course,' said the Frenchman, 'you would push it. Naturally.'

'As soon as the hydrogen was detected, all the governments throughout the world were immediately notified of the situation,' I continued.

'Bloody well right,' snorted the big Australian.

'However, since then it has been discovered that the hydrogen is evaporating . . .'

'Evaporating?' interrupted the Oriental gentleman.

'Correct. It would appear that bursts of particles from the Sun are heating up, thereby causing it to evaporate. It seems that the Yela, finding the Sun still too active, has abandoned the present attempt to destroy the Earth.'

'How do you know the Yela has gone,' asked another Oriental gentleman, 'assuming it was there in the first place?'

'We have a report to this effect,' I replied, 'from Betelgeuse's fleet, which has been stationed out beyond Pluto for several years.'

'Why haven't they been in touch with us before now?' asked a Russian general.

'Up until now all radio communication with space has been inoperative.'

'We gave no permission for radio jamming,' exclaimed the American.

'Neither did we,' said the Russian general.

'The communication difficulty was a natural phenomenon,' I explained.

'I think it is about time we taught the Yela a lesson,' said a German.

'How are you going to do that?' rumbled the Russian.

'Destroy it. Hunt it down and strike before it has a chance to return and attempt another attack on the Earth,' replied the German.

'How do you know it'll come back?' asked another Oriental gentleman.

'He doesn't,' boomed a voice from the back. 'We could find no evidence to support this eccentric theory about hydrogen.'

'Leave it alone, Dr Nk, we know that none of your radio telescopes works,' said the English military gentleman.

'I think the Germans could have a valid point,' remarked the slender Italian.

'What about?' asked the American.

'The point about the Yela returning,' replied the Italian.

'Why should it return? It has been defeated. For the second time, too. It'd be crazy to try again,' said the American.

'The Yela knows this planet is inhabited and that we are alien to it. It would be unwise not to consider that it might attack again,' I insisted.

The American glared at me.

'There is no hydrogen,' shouted Dr Nk from the back of the room.

'I would have thought it would try again. It is only a

matter of time before the bombardment of interplanetary space by streams of particles from the Sun comes to an end. Once things are back to normal the hydrogen won't evaporate any more and the Earth will then be in danger,' I concluded.

'How come there are all these particles flying around at the moment?' asked the American.

'The after-effect of the lithium bomb.'

'Then we could drop another one.'

'We could, but there is always the danger that radiation levels here on Earth would become lethal.'

'So what is to be done now?' asked a fair-haired, tall Norwegian.

'It is obvious we must attack first,' came the leathery comment from an Israeli.

This last remark brought the assembly to an abrupt halt. They all looked at each other.

I waited for some reaction with growing curiosity.

'How would you propose to attack?' asked the Russian general, immediately throwing the ball back into Israel's court.

'Attack. Seek out the enemy and destroy him,' responded the Israeli blandly.

'Very commendable. Israel has only a few ships. We have many that could be lost in such a fight. So you lose little and we lose much. Is it not so?' said the elderly Frenchman.

'Whatever you do, we will take *our* ships and seek out the enemy,' growled the Israeli.

'That would be pure suicide,' commented the English military man.

At this point the V.I.P.s broke up into groups, which gradually developed into two distinct huddles. Meanwhile the Israeli simply rocked backwards and forwards on a chair with a smile cracking his bronzed face from time to time.

'If this is the case, we shall fight with all our might to defeat the evil one,' came a distant voice.

'How much hydrogen did you say you'd seen?' asked another muffled voice.

'10^{15} tons,' I shouted.

'What I can't understand is how so much hydrogen can be in space. Perhaps God has something to do with it,' went on the voice.

'Gentlemen,' announced the American at length, 'it has been decided that we send all available ships into space to seek out and destroy the Yela.'

The Israeli applauded vigorously at this point.

'The Americans and the Israelis are in league to get us to send our ships into space to be destroyed,' exclaimed an Arab.

'Our ships are just as vulnerable as yours,' countered the American.

'Yes, but you will keep some ships in reserve so that when all ours are lost you will still hold the balance of power,' responded the Arab.

'I agree with the Americans. We should send up the whole fleet,' concluded the Russian general, with an air of God-given certainty.

'Dr Newman, we think your brief is then clear. All available ships are to proceed into deep space in pursuit of the enemy. When the enemy has been sought out, he must be destroyed,' instructed the American and the Russian general.

Newman nodded, with his eyes seemingly focused at infinity.

'There is . . .' he tried to say.

'You know, Ivan,' said the American as they started to file out of the office, 'I think we should have meetings like this more often.'

Newman continued to stand there with a completely blank face. For a moment I wondered whether he'd suffered some internal disorder. Then he moaned, 'Get the whole fleet out into space. In five minutes. That's what they want me to do.'

With this pronouncement he heaved himself over to the communications console.

'Yes,' I agreed, 'that's what they want.' Then, not wanting to become caught up in the forthcoming administrative holocaust, I left Newman's office at a brisk pace.

The landing strips were clearing fast. Vehicles were now taking off continuously as I crossed from the administration building to my own office.

'I hear the terrestrial white fathers have committed their entire space fleet to defeating the Yela,' said Betelgeuse from behind my desk as I walked in. He was smoking what I supposed would be one of his last cigars.

'Yes, a decision based upon what are known as political realities. How is the news from space?'

'The Yela seems to have left the solar system. But their move could be only a feint.'

'Have you changed your plans?'

'Perhaps a little. My first reaction was to go in the opposite direction to the Yela. But now I am curious to see what happens to this great armada of Earth ships if and when it catches up with the Yela.'

Here with a grunt and a grimace Betelgeuse flung his cigar out of an open window.

'That I think would be interesting,' I said.

'So you will come with us after all?'

'Maybe I will. On condition you agree to transfer me to one of the Earth ships at the end. How much d'you really know about the Yela?'

'Its territory is enormous. Virtually the whole of Ursa Major. How it guards it, I don't know. What it looks like, I don't know. There is no account of anyone ever having seen one of its spaceships, let alone the actual Yela.'

'Which way has the creature gone?'

'A heat path has been detected pointing in the direction of Centaurus.'

'Strange, I would have thought it would have travelled

directly towards Ursa Major,' I said, reaching for an astronomical map of the night sky.

'Ursa Major lies approximately 10 hours 40 minutes right ascension at 56 degrees north declination. Whereas Centaurus lies 13 hours right ascension, 50 degrees south declination,' stated Betelgeuse.

'What's attractive about Centaurus? It would be an awfully long way round to get back to Ursa Major.'

'That's why I said the move might only be a feint.'

'How far is Centaurus?'

'The nearest star in Centaurus is some three light-years away.'

'Is there anything of special importance there?'

'Let me see, what do I know about the region? The bright star Alpha Centauri is rather like your own Sun. From what I remember it is interesting because it is a multiple star with two components. One component is the same colour as the Sun, but its mass is 9 percent greater, and its radius is 23 percent larger, and it is 50 percent brighter. The other component is somewhat redder than the Sun. Slightly smaller than the Sun, and it goes around the first component once every 80 years.'

'Sounds as though you've been there.'

'No,' smiled Betelgeuse. 'No, that's just information from the computer. The computer states that there is very little chance of life existing in that region.'

'Why would that be?'

'In our experience multiple star systems don't have planetary systems.'

'How accurately can the direction of the Yela ship be determined?'

'Fairly accurately. So long as the heat trail doesn't cool off.'

'What reason have you for thinking the Yela's move might be a trick of some kind?'

'Well, the departure of the Yela in such a hurry is

unprecedented. I did a computer check on its behaviour, and this sudden move is not typical of it.'

'Which suggests to me that the move is *not* a trick.'

'Perhaps something very unexpected has happened then.'

'That could well be so,' I agreed. 'And I suppose you'd like to find out what,' I added.

'Correct. My curiosity is now aroused. Why should the Yela have left in a hurry, and why in the direction of Centaurus? There is a mystery for you.'

With a light tap on the door, my old friend Colonel Rhodes popped his head into the room.

'Am I intruding?'

'Not at all, Colonel.'

'Betelgeuse! Haven't seen you for years.'

'They work you damned hard,' replied Betelgeuse.

'Your English has improved.'

'I get a lot of practice.'

'You know, I shall never forget you fishing Dick and me out of space, after our ship was blown up in the first attack wave of the Yela.'

'Dick took it very well, but you thought we were the Yela. You should have seen your face.'

'You would probably be more than a little perturbed if you thought you were being picked up by a Yela ship,' said Rhodes with a grin.

'That is true. I suppose we all have preconceived ideas concerning the unknown. What has interested me in getting to know Earth people better is the amount of superstition that surrounds all your ideas and beliefs.'

'Don't you have superstitions?' I asked.

'I suppose we did back in our primitive state.'

'You're superstitious over the Yela?' said the Colonel.

'Not superstitious, just frightened. I've seen too much destroyed by that creature not to fear it.'

'You say creature?'

'It is a bad word. Words by their very nature are semantic.'

'Meaning what?' persisted Rhodes.

'A creature, literally, is anything created, whether animate or inanimate,' replied Betelgeuse thoughtfully. 'I should have studied semasiology. It would have been most useful in talking to Earth people.'

'What is semasiology?' I asked.

'It is a branch of philology which deals with the meaning of words.'

'You must have a very receptive memory. A bit like blotting paper, I shouldn't wonder,' remarked Rhodes.

'I fear not. My memory is a photographic one. Once seen, always remembered. Over the years I have developed this type of memory to save time when hunting for references or diagrams.'

'Changing the subject,' said the Colonel, 'I hear the balloon has gone up.'

'You've had orders?' I asked.

'Yep. We leave in about two hours. Sealed orders to be opened when we get to our first rendezvous point.'

'Those sealed orders are probably just a sheet of blank paper at the moment,' said Betelgeuse.

'Why?'

'Because the authorities have no idea of what to do if they get their fleet to a rendezvous point.'

'I'm not with you.' Rhodes looked puzzled.

'Have you had any instructions concerning the intense radiation you'll be certain to encounter?'

'No.'

'Well, then, let me give you a piece of advice,' grunted Betelgeuse. 'Unless you get yourself some solid protection, there's not much chance of your reaching any rendezvous point.'

'A good tipoff, Betelgeuse. Thanks. I'll get myself over to stores and collect some heavy space suits. Excuse me,' said Rhodes, heading for the door.

'By the way, where is the rendezvous point?' asked Betelgeuse.

'The far side of Jupiter.'

'Will you get clearance for our takeoff?' Betelgeuse asked, as soon as Rhodes had gone. 'I want priority,' he added.

Newman proved difficult when I asked for a top-class priority clearance. Not only that, but he was unhappy about my going with Betelgeuse – I had the distinct feeling that he didn't really trust Betelgeuse. It took a lot of coaxing, and threatening, before I could obtain his signature for our departure.

'You'll live to regret it,' were his last words to me.

'Ready?' asked Alcyone who was waiting outside Newman's office.

'I think so.'

'Good. Betelgeuse is already on the launch pad.'

'Anything the matter?' I asked as we strode towards the ship.

'Sometimes one's innermost thoughts are sad,' she quietly replied.

We walked on in silence. Betelgeuse's ship was like a mountain. By comparison with Earth ships it was enormous, standing fully a thousand metres high. We stepped onto the external lift, which was soon propelling us skywards. I took a last look round at the blue sky and sea and the yellows and reds of the land and then walked into the ship through the airlock doors.

The most noticeable thing about it was, first, the feeling of space; second, the lack of clutter – Earth vehicles were usually crammed with equipment. This ship seemed simplicity itself. It was, of course, constructed as a separate entity, controlling its own destiny, like an island universe. In contrast our Earth ships still relied heavily on a ground computer to deal with all really serious emergencies.

'Welcome aboard,' came Rigel's greeting.

'I see you've been doing some redecoration.'

I glanced over the mat metal finish of the walls.

'Your quarters are on F deck. It's not too noisy,' Rigel said.

We descended in the lift to deck F and stepped out into a corridor encircling the lift shaft. From this round corridor ran four straight ones at right angles to the lift shaft. Alcyone moved a few feet down one of the latter and opened a door. Inside was a pleasant room with bathroom and galley on one side and sleeping quarters on the other.

'This was Betelgeuse's cabin,' said Alcyone, poking her head into all the nooks and crannies.

'I would appreciate it if you would remove your luggage from the flight deck. We depart in half an hour,' boomed Betelgeuse's voice over the intercom.

Alcyone and I made a couple of trips to the flight deck and had managed to stow away most of our belongings before Betelgeuse's voice boomed again. 'Attention, please. Five minutes to takeoff. I repeat, five minutes to departure.'

We returned quickly upwards again.

'Everything O.K.?' asked Betelgeuse as we came out of the lift.

'Fine. Thank you for the cabin,' I said.

'Well, we are next to go,' said Betelgeuse, switching on the radio receivers.

'Nine . . . eight . . . seven . . . six . . . five . . . first engine on ascent,' crackled a voice over the radio. Our ship seemed to shiver for a moment. 'Beautiful . . . twenty-six . . . little pitch over, very good,' continued the voice enthusiastically.

'We go in two minutes,' said Betelgeuse.

Alcyone and I pulled seats from the wall and strapped ourselves into them.

'A little bit of slow wallowing. Pings, aggs and misfin all agree,' said the voice over the radio.

'Blue leader, this is mission control, over.'

'Blue leader, you are zero minus 50, over.'

'Counting,' replied Betelgeuse, and set the computer for takeoff.

A digital counter above the control console showed the last seconds ticking away before takeoff.

'Everybody ready?' asked Betelgeuse. Everybody nodded as he looked round at his crew.

'Blue leader, you are zero minus ten . . . nine . . . eight . . . seven . . . six . . . you have ignition.'

The floor beneath my feet pressed upwards as millions of pounds of thrust seized the ship. Betelgeuse turned on the outside visual scanners. The ship gathered momentum. I watched the Earth receding. For a brief moment I wondered what the future might hold in store for us, but not in my wildest thoughts could I have come remotely near the truth.

4 The Voyage Begins

Acceleration forces crushed our soft body tissues deep into the seats. This first part of our journey still had to be made using chemical fuel, a wasteful and messy procedure. But soon the chemical jets reached terminal velocity. For a moment we lay motionless on our seats, the fierce pressure having eased into a weightless condition.

'Everyone up. Magnetosphere approaching,' cried Betelgeuse, adjusting the rotary sensors of the ship to combat the weightlessness. He then moved over to where the space suits were stored.

'You're in a hell of a hurry,' I said.

'No time to waste. We've got a lot of travelling to do.'

'I thought we were just going to the far side of Jupiter,' said Alcyone, fighting to get her suit on.

'We don't have time to bother about any rendezvous or about any discussions on what to do next.'

'Where are we going, then?'

'Our fleet is already on its way towards Alpha Centauri, in pursuit of the Yela.'

'It's nice to know there's someone around to make the decisions,' I muttered as I flopped to the floor in my efforts to force myself into the space suit I was holding.

'We'll get out beyond the asteroid belt before we sort out a comfortable pressure for the ship,' grinned Betelgeuse, amused at my struggles.

At last I got myself into the suit, but for a while I felt too exhausted to get up. When eventually I did manage to stagger to my feet the heavy suit pulled me downwards and outwards in a curious way.

'Lead woven into a mixture of fibreglass and beryllium,' explained Betelgeuse, helping me on with the helmet. When it was in position he gave a hefty thump, which seated it onto the suit-fixing ring. I fastened the securing clips, put on my boots and gloves, and flopped down again.

'Are you comfortable?' chuckled Alcyone as she helped me to my feet and over the floor towards our seats.

Suddenly there came a deafening explosion. The floor of the flight deck became dislodged from my feet and I felt the rim of my visor hit the edge of the seat. The babbling I heard eventually turned into Betelgeuse's voice ordering an immediate check on all the ship's systems.

'Are we being shot at?' I asked, gaining the security of my seat.

'There's no apparent damage,' Rigel informed us, as he looked over the computer printout, 'but the outer skin took a sharp increase of temperature.'

I was just about to look towards Alcyone to see that she was all right when a second explosion threw us all into an untidy heap of shining arms and legs and dented helmets. Rigel was the first to move, making his way across the floor back to the computer. I caught a glimpse of Betelgeuse's worried face as he heaved his body over mine and struggled upright.

'No damage reported. But it looks as if there was a high electrical discharge measured this time,' said Rigel.

'Electrical discharge?' queried Betelgeuse.

'The radioactivity level has risen to danger level,' continued Rigel.

'Let's hope these suits work,' I grunted and climbed back onto my seat.

'I want an analysis of what's happening on the skin of the ship,' instructed Betelgeuse. 'Dick, get the life-support systems ready.'

This order spurred me into activity.

'There's a steady buildup of positive electric charge on the outer skin,' Rigel announced.

'Triboelectricity,' I grunted, as I carried the last of the life-support systems into the cabin.

'That could be it,' nodded Rigel, swinging on his pack.

'A terrific buildup of positive charge on the outer surface of the ship. Then suddenly a big electric current starts to flow, leading to an explosion of magnetic forces,' I added.

Betelgeuse and Rigel began desperately trying to find a way to prevent a third explosion.

'Switch off all electrical supplies,' Betelgeuse called out.

Immediately everything went dark and silent – except for the thumping of my own heart. After a moment or two the silence began to trouble me. There should still be voice communication, using the radio packs in our suits. 'Fool,' I swore to myself, switching on a small button at the side of my helmet.

'How much longer before we're through the magneto-sphere?' I heard Alcyone asking.

'Only a few minutes,' replied Betelgeuse.

Faintly on my headphones I could hear a distant instruction, 'This is red leader to red fleet, report all damage. Red leader to all red fleet, report your damage ...' the voice continued.

Suddenly there was a monstrous blue-green flash followed by another deafening roar. The strange light lasted only a fraction of a second, just long enough to illuminate the cabin. I shook my head, trying to rid myself of a sound in my ears like that of tearing cloth.

'Everyone all right?' I heard Betelgeuse's voice, as though inside some vast hall. One by one we replied that we were still O.K. Then Rigel somehow managed to get to the console and to re-establish the power supply, and the total blackout returned slowly to artificial daylight.

'All systems O.K., but damage reported on outer skin.'

'Bad?' asked Betelgeuse.

'Some loss of material due to evaporation by extreme heating.'

'Radiation level?'

'Safe now,' said Rigel, putting down the printouts he was consulting.

'We'll remain in our suits until after our course change.'

'How long are we to go on accelerating?' I asked.

'It will be best not to adjust the ship's internal pressure until we're under the ION drive,' muttered Betelgeuse, ignoring my question.

'You mean we're going to go on accelerating all the time?' I persisted.

'Certainly,' replied Rigel.

Slowly it penetrated my thick skull that this wasn't just a solar system exercise. This was a space voyage. The thought both excited and frightened me.

Once Betelgeuse had made his pressure adjustment and conditions were tolerably comfortable again, I started a long study of the functionings of the ship systems. It was vital to everyone on board that each of us should be mentally equipped to save the lives of the others should danger threaten. For this it was essential to have an intimate knowledge of every detail of the ship's construction. Of course we all relied heavily on the computer, which monitored the functioning of the various systems, making automatic adjustments to them according to the instructions of a master program that even Rigel was loath to interfere with.

Life in space wasn't as companionable as I'd imagined it might be. A cyclical rota was drawn up requiring each of us to carry out a duty watch of about two hours' duration. If one continued to divide time into 'days' of twenty-four hours, there were approximately four such cycles per day, giving each of us three 'free' periods of about six hours in which to sleep, read and relax. I soon came to realize that this rigid schedule helped to preserve sanity – although to begin with, it seemed unnecessarily regimented.

The rota for the duty cycle was Alcyone first, me second, followed by Betelgeuse and Rigel. As I took my turn in the first cycle, a digital clock above the control console told me how long we'd been on our journey. We were now $T+6$ hours. The others had left it to me so that right from the beginning I would get accustomed to running the ship without having someone looking over my shoulder. This I appreciated, but within minutes of my taking watch the silence brought on a wave of loneliness.

Alcyone had left a very small electronic receiver on the console. I had noticed the others carrying similar devices about with them all the time. The small box was just a signalling device operated by the computer. Every time the computer made a calculation, the little box would bleep. I connected a cord into my earphone set, placing the box in a pocket of my space suit. The bleeper was obviously a simple but effective way of making sure no one went to sleep while on watch. No more pinching oneself in order to stay awake. I sat down at the console and reflected on how very uncomfortable these heavy space suits were.

Without warning there came a loud bleep in my ear. I eased myself over to the printout. Sure enough a few seconds later the computer divulged what it had been up to. Silent keys inside the machine typed out a series of mathematical notations. My job now was to find out what all these numbers meant. For this purpose Alcyone had left me an instruction manual. I started to run my eye down columns of symbols.

The information which the computer had just given me turned out to be data relating to the quantity of urine converted back into its original chemical constituents. The recycling of the life-support system in Betelgeuse's ship was designed for space flights of very long duration. Nothing was wasted. Everything was used and reused.

After the excitement of the first bleep nothing further

happened. I occupied the remainder of my watch studying the column of symbols in the ship's manual.

'All quiet?' asked Betelgeuse, stepping from the lift.

'Yes, except for a quantity of reconstituted urine.'

'Very important,' he said and sat down next to me.

'It's amazing how quiet it becomes up here when one's left alone.'

'Sometimes it can be very noisy. Take our nursery ships, for instance. Tens of children rushing around the decks.'

'How do the crew stand it?'

'It is a duty. We all go through it at some time in our lives. Just as I have served in school ships. Everyone is expected to make his or her contribution towards the perpetuation of our people. I must admit that there are usually more women on the nursery ships than men.'

'I would have thought that a woman would want to look after her own children.'

'They don't have any of their own as you do on Earth. In space it is important to produce exactly the right number of the species. Because of strains on our resources of food, water and energy, it is crucial to avoid the evils of overpopulation. And it is also important for every member of the fleet to be active at all times, women as well as men.'

'You produce the children artificially?'

'Perhaps artificially to you, but there is nothing artificial about eggs and sperm combining together to produce life.'

I now understood why Alcyone had never bothered with the problem of becoming pregnant. She was sterile. Her eggs, collected sometime during her life, were kept elsewhere for procreation.

'How do you select children for, say, a job like yours?'

'The same as you do on Earth.'

'You don't select a child and bring it up to be a doctor or an engineer, or to be the leader?'

'There is no leader in our society. I just happened to be

the first ship that came along when you were blown up in space. It might very well have been any one of our people – Aldebaran, Belatrix, Censa or Canopus.'

'How do you make decisions among yourselves?'

'Everybody of adequate experience casts a vote.'

'Very much like democratic societies on Earth,' I suggested.

'Except there are fewer of us. No such system would be workable for hundreds of millions of people. Nothing but blind stumblings could result from it – just the way it is on Earth,' came Betelgeuse's grim reply.

'The decision to follow the Yela was made on a vote,' he went on. 'Not everyone wanted to go, but a majority wished to do so.'

'The others could then go off and do something on their own?'

'They certainly could, but that would be very foolish, for then the life expectancy would drop dramatically. The chance of survival becomes small for anyone who leaves the protection of the main fleet.'

Betelgeuse leaned over the computer printout, anticipating the bleep by a second or so. 'We're entering the asteroid belt,' he said, tearing the paper from the machine and reading, apparently for my benefit, 'a multitude of small celestial bodies moving in orbits mostly between Mars and Jupiter.'

Some minutes later Betelgeuse typed instructions into the computer. A large screen immediately behind the console lit up revealing a beautiful coloured picture of Mars. The most noticeable parts of the planet were the white polar caps, the dust-swept plains and a truly massive volcano. On this occasion everything was clearly visible. At other times the whole surface could be obscured by violent dust storms.

'I wouldn't enjoy a tour of duty on that fellow,' I remarked. 'It's not too bad in the daytime, at least on the equator, where the temperature may reach 70 degrees

Fahrenheit. But at night it can drop as much as 140 degrees. On the polar caps there can be 200 degrees of frost.'

'What is the pressure of the atmosphere?' asked Betelgeuse.

'Only about one-half of one percent of that of the Earth.'

'What is the white material on the polar caps?'

'Water vapor and carbon dioxide condensed out of the atmosphere as a thin frost. When the temperature rises, the frost sublimes directly into water vapor. I suppose it's the lack of rain and the absence of oceans and rivers that make the surface so very different from that of the Earth. On Earth, the water coming from the mountains splits the plateaux with canyons. It both creates and wears down irregularities and it shapes coastlines, filling in low-lying areas with sediment. On the Earth water is the dominating agency, whereas on Mars the wind is all-powerful. It picks up the dust and uses it like sandpaper to wear down the topography.'

'Yet there appear to be canyon-like details,' said Betelgeuse thoughtfully, pointing to the sides of a long straight groove. 'These would surely indicate the presence of rivers?'

'At one time there may have been, but there are none today.'

'I would expect asteroids of water ice would sometimes hit the planet,' continued Betelgeuse. 'Then for a time at least there would be a flow of rivers, as on Earth.'

'That is very possible,' I agreed.

The computer bleeped. The ship rolled, there was sudden acceleration, then the ship was steady again.

'Asteroid,' Betelgeuse grunted laconically.

I clambered off my seat, gave Betelgeuse a pat on the shoulder and made my way clumsily to my cabin.

It was dark inside except for a small table light. By it I found a note from Alcyone. On looking round I saw that she was sound asleep on her bunk. By the note was a capsule and a cup of water. The note told me I was to take the pill and then to get some rest. However, lying on my bunk in the uncomfortable space suit seemed to make my wakefulness more acute.

'Come on, you lazy thing,' I heard Alcyone's voice in my earphones.

'But I've hardly been asleep,' I grumbled, keeping my eyes closed against the glaring light from the cabin.

'You've been out for a good fifteen hours,' she said, swinging my legs off the bunk. 'Your turn for duty now.'

'Anything happen?' I asked, trying to rub my eyes through my visor.

'Jupiter is coming up large and clear.'

'Any news from the Earth fleet?'

'From a babble of chitchat I gather nobody quite knows what anyone else is doing. It also seems that some ships were lost coming up through the magnetosphere.'

'Destroyed?'

'Apparently, yes. Rigel thinks the electrical disturbances might have triggered off armed torpedoes.'

'But why carry armed torpedoes on takeoff?'

'It would be likely to happen in the confusion, I think. Before you go on duty it would be good to accustom yourself to the galley.'

The galley was more like a sterilized operating theatre than a kitchen. A large table with benches affixed to it provided plenty of sitting area. Food was dispensed from a cylinder in the middle of the table.

'Three thousand beautiful calories. A well-balanced diet for a growing spaceman,' Alcyone said, handing me a few dried-up leaves.

'Good old synthetic food washed down with reconstituted waste. Commonly known as vintage H_2O.'

'Correct.'

'No salt and pepper?'

'You are criticizing the way I make the food,' she said, tapping the container.

'What's the culinary name?' I asked holding up a piece of leaf.

'Medium-level mixture.'

'Looks like small pieces of tobacco leaf.'

Seeing that no prime rib would be forthcoming on this journey, I left Alcyone to her job in the galley. Still encumbered by the heavy suit, I made my way as best I could to the flight deck. There I found the computer spewing out vast quantities of numerical material. I grabbed the manual and searched for a key to the message. Unfortunately there didn't seem to be any suitable instruction anywhere in the manual. As more and more paper was disgorged by the printer, a sense of panic overwhelmed me. I felt sure the ship must be in serious trouble.

'Alcyone,' I called, 'the computer's got a case of mathematical diarrhoea which I don't understand.'

'Coming,' she said in her singsong way. Arriving a few moments later, she shuffled across to the computer.

'No wonder,' she announced after studying the information for a moment. 'It's a message from one of our ships in high-level code. I must hand this to Betelgeuse immediately.'

The remainder of my second watch was uneventful. I continued to instruct myself on the ways of the computer and also took a brief look at the external communication system. In addition to the usual radio links I found that under certain circumstances it was possible to generate an outgoing laser beam to be used for transmission only.

'Sorry about this,' said Betelgeuse, arriving at the lift door and waving the message. 'I should have told you I was expecting it.'

'That's all right. It did take me by surprise though.'

'And you concluded that the ship was a total malfunction?'

'I did. Good news from your fleet?'

'They calculate that we should catch up with them at approximately $T+2000$.'

'About three months,' I mused.

'The calculation really starts from the time we make our course change round Jupiter.'

'Once we leave Jupiter I assume we'll be on the ION powered engines.'

'Correct.'

The computer rattled and I took the paper it ejected. 'According to this there are fast-moving objects in front of and behind us,' I said.

'Probably asteroids.'

'No, these are objects producing a fair amount of heat.'

Betelgeuse turned on the outside monitors, and instantly on the screen behind the console came a picture of Earth ships all around us.

'How the devil did they come to be there?' exclaimed Betelgeuse in some irritation. 'They must pretty well have exhausted all their chemical fuel supply.'

He quickly typed a message for the computer. 'This is blue leader calling, this is blue leader calling, over.'

'Hello, blue leader, this is red fox, over,' came a voice at length, crackling on the loudspeakers and in our headphones.

'Hello, red fox,' said Betelgeuse, as we watched one of the visual monitors home in on the ship we were communicating with. 'Can you tell me for how long you burnt your engines?'

'Blue leader, can't tell you exactly, but it seemed a fair old while. You set off like the clappers of hell. We had to keep burning to catch up with you,' cried the elated voice.

'Thank you, red fox, over and out,' answered Betelgeuse. Turning to me, he muttered, 'Seems a strange thing to do.'

'What, to follow you?'

'Yes. I have a nasty suspicion that . . .' Betelgeuse began. Opening a small locker, he went on, 'I took the trouble to collect a mission-control operations envelope.'

'Blank piece of paper?'

'We'll see,' he said opening the envelope.

'Damn their impudence,' he roared, after reading a single sheet. 'These orders state that the Earth fleet in conjunction with my fleet is to hunt down and destroy Yela ships wherever and whenever the Yela is contacted.'

'No wonder those fellows gave chase.'

'Yes, and everyone up here will be following us. They'll be burning up their fuel at a prodigious rate.'

'Do those ships really have the staying power for a deep-space voyage?'

'Not over any extended period. Five years would be a maximum, I would think. They are very overcrowded.'

'What I was thinking about was the life-support systems. Will they last a five-year journey?'

'Oh yes. The ships should have been modified to take on much longer-duration journeys. Their life-support systems are very similar to the one in this ship. As long as there is power, the support systems will continue to function. What they don't have are the finer engineering points that make deep-space travel less irksome.'

'How do you mean?'

'They have no proper rotational sensor control. Those ships have to be flown at set speeds to create certain g forces. On this ship we control the pressure internally to a very fine degree.'

'Why isn't our system operating correctly at present?'

'Because a lot of drive would be wasted correcting pressure changes due to chance happenings, like the one we experienced in the asteroid belt.'

'What else don't they have?'

'They certainly don't have the kind of recreational facilities we have here. It is very important if one is to spend a large part of one's life in space to be able to study, read and learn new things.'

'It looks as though it's going to be a rough trip for them.'

'For us all, I think,' said Betelgeuse quietly.

5   In Pursuit of the Yela

At T+34 everyone was on the flight deck. Jupiter covered the vision monitor. However many times one sees this enormous planet of hydrogen, methane and ammonia, it always looks evil, especially as one approaches the solid, forbidding core lying a thousand miles below the swirling, racing clouds of ammonia crystals.

'This is blue leader to all red foxes,' said Betelgeuse. 'This is blue leader to all red foxes. I have calculated the point where you are to enter the cloud structure of Jupiter. It is of the utmost importance to keep accurately to the flight path. A deviation of a degree at your exit will put you a light-year away from our destination point. Stand by for technical instructions.'

We all listened, but there was no reply from the accompanying fleet of ships.

'Three minutes to course change,' exclaimed Rigel, going to his seat. Without hesitation we all did the same, strapping ourselves in firmly.

Every second we approached closer to the swirling clouds, which now filled the monitor screen. I could just make out a couple of Earth ships as vague shapes in the haze directly in front of us. For a sickening moment I had the thought that we were on a collision course. Then the g forces started building to a screaming agony as the ship swept on its tangential path past Jupiter. Although this type of course change was new to me, I could see vast possibilities in the method. In deep-space travel the gravitational field of a star could be used in a similar way to great advantage.

The g forces lessened at last as we came clear of the clouds. Once again out in front of us were the black depths of space, but the stars ahead had changed.

'That was most satisfactory,' muttered Betelgeuse, as he eased himself out of his suit.

'It's always pleasant to have a helping hand,' agreed Rigel.

It wasn't only the free boost to our journey which elated me. It was also the removal of our space suits. The freedom with which I could move my limbs was totally sensual.

'Well, we can now get down to the serious part of our journey. Rigel, I'm sure Dick here would appreciate the gravitational pressure he's used to on Earth.'

'Coming up right away,' said Rigel, punching the information for the computer.

'And you can start full I O N power,' Betelgeuse added as he stretched himself luxuriously.

The return to normal forces made me temporarily light-headed.

'What does our course look like?' asked Alcyone.

'According to this,' I replied, holding up the printout as it came through, 'we are headed towards 14 hours 29 minutes right ascension, 60 degrees 23 minutes south declination.'

'That puts us practically dead on course,' remarked Alcyone.

'But surely this is the position of Alpha Centauri taken from Earth.'

'Yes,' replied Alcyone, 'I have based all our flight plan on the Earth and solar system, our known points of reference.'

'Red leader calling blue leader, where the hell are you? Over,' suddenly crackled a voice from the loudspeakers.

'Red leader, this is blue leader. We are on course: 14 hours 30 minutes right ascension, 60 degrees 25 minutes south declination, as observed from Earth. Over.'

'Someone has made a right mess of this one,' came the reply.

'Blue leader calling W.S.HQ. mission control,' said Betelgeuse. 'This is blue leader calling mission control, over.'

'Hello, blue leader, what is your problem? Over,' said a distant voice after a long delay.

'Mission control. Request an immediate navigational check on all ships, over.'

'Roger, over and out.'

'Blue leader, this is red fox 224, can you help?' came another voice.

'This is blue leader, what is your difficulty, red fox 224? Over.'

'We appear to be lost,' came the plaintive reply. 'Over.'

'Red fox 224. This is blue leader. Suggest you call mission control and sort yourself out. Over and out,' growled Betelgeuse irritably. 'Rigel, launch the navigational instruments,' he added.

A second or so later I saw on the screen two small metal canisters float away from the side of the ship, one to the left, the other to the right.

'Set the telescopes to receive beacons from Earth tracking stations,' instructed Betelgeuse.

'Blue leader, this is mission control. Over.'

'Mission control, this is blue leader. Over.'

'It looks as though the fleet is spread over the sky from 9 to 15 hours right ascension and anything from 32 degrees to 70 degrees south declination, over.'

'Thank you, mission control, over and out. Red leader, this is blue leader. Did you hear that? Over.'

'Yes, blue leader. It will take time to correct the mistake, with speed 22,150 kilometres per second. Over.'

'This is blue leader. Our rendezvous point will be at T+2000 hours, on course 14 hours 30 minutes RA, 60 degrees 25 minutes SD. Over.'

'Message understood. Rendezvous at T+2000 hours. See you there. Over and out.'

'Idiots. What do they think this is, a space Grand Prix on a public holiday?'

'I've got a fix on the Earth beacons: 14 hours 27 minutes RA, 60 degrees 24 minutes SD,' announced Rigel.

'Set up course-correction procedure. Then get those front telescopes tracking on Alpha Centauri.'

'What about the rear telescopes?' asked Rigel.

'Better set them on the Sun,' said Betelgeuse thoughtfully.

'Why the Sun?' I asked.

'By measuring the displacement of the iron lines of the spectrum, the computer can calculate the distance we are from the Sun,' explained Rigel.

'What is the purpose of the telescopes?' I asked.

'The two forward facing telescopes are placed about 5 kilometres apart. They are focused on a star and they automatically track on that star – Alpha Centauri in this case. The optical light received by each telescope is converted into an electrical current. The computer then compares the two currents in such a way as to give us an accurate fix on our destination,' said Alcyone.

'How accurate?'

'Within one ten-thousandth of an arc second.'

'Damned good. Not much chance of going adrift with that order of precision.'

'Talking of going adrift, it is recorded that in the early history of our space wanderings such disasters actually happened. That was why we were led to develop accurate interferometric methods of guidance,' remarked Betelgeuse.

'In the very early days they travelled long distances in a frozen state,' Alcyone said. 'They'd set themselves on course and then freeze themselves. You can imagine what happened when they woke up thirty years later to find only a dark hole in space.'

'Why did you stop freezing yourselves?'

'It was discovered that it disrupted body functions, and who wants to live forever?' said Alcyone cheerfully.

'Flights often last for hundreds of years,' added Rigel, 'with each new generation recording its own life cycle. It is even recorded, many thousands of years ago, that our fleet went off to explore the far side of the galaxy.'

'But that's an enormous journey. How long did it take?'

'At the speeds we can achieve today, it would take twenty thousand years,' answered Rigel.

'Incredible. It still amazes me that this ship can achieve a velocity close on a fifth the speed of light. No Earth person would have conceived ten years ago that this would be possible. It's a completely new dimension of space technology.'

As the hours ticked slowly by I grew steadily more accustomed to space routine. The watch on the functioning of the ship went on meticulously. The complex systems were all apparently in first-class order. The spare hours were filled with sleep, since I found myself quite exhausted after each watch. For the others, sleep didn't come easily, however. Their wakefulness arose, it seemed, from a highly developed sixth sense, an alertness to detect instantly any serious malfunction.

T+100 came and went, followed by 200, 300 and 400. Although little seemed to happen, time passed remorselessly away.

It was shortly after taking over control at T+1474 that I became conscious of a physiological change taking place in all of us. For me, sleep seemed to have vanished almost as though I were taking drugs to keep me awake. For several duty cycles I hadn't taken much notice of this change. But now I saw an opposite kind of behaviour in Alcyone. She was coming off watch and sleeping without the help of the pills she'd been taking. The relentless buildup of strain I'd noticed in Betelgeuse and Rigel was slipping away from their faces. A kind of inversion seemed to be occurring. While the others were becoming more relaxed I was becoming taut, almost to the point of panic.

After each turn on watch I would go to my bunk. Half an hour later I was still wide awake. To induce sleep and reduce the feeling of tiredness I turned in desperation to pill-taking, which is something I do only very rarely. Still no sleep seemed to be forthcoming, only a slight diminution in the mounting panic.

After several hundred hours my body screamed for rest, while my brain kept on issuing orders to my aching limbs. On watch I began hearing noises. At first I thought one of the others was just moving about. When I discovered this wasn't the case, strange formless thoughts suffused my mind. I developed a dread that the ship was haunted. Sometimes the inner casing would move very slightly and, as it did so, it created a muffled tapping noise. I would switch on the outside vision monitors to see who was knocking to be let in. I knew it to be a creature of surprising horror whose form must never be allowed to enter by consciousness.

Then I imagined I could hear the scratching of rats. In what seemed a blinding moment of perception I convinced myself that the ship was also rat-infested. Whenever I felt I wasn't being watched by the others I set about exploring, to seek out and destroy the rats. It was while I was on one of these sorties that I suddenly knew I was being watched, not by one of the others, but by the nameless horror which had sought to enter the ship. Somehow the thing must have found a way inside. This notion hit me while I was searching the engineering shop, close by the main propulsion unit and nuclear reactor.

At this point something cleared in my mind, as if a new circuit were suddenly activated, one which permitted me to observe myself from outside. The outsider simply noted that I was suffering from insomnia and must relax in order to banish a lot of silly hallucinations. It was the first time in hundreds of hours that I began to feel at peace. The slow realization that I'd been driving myself to death just because I couldn't sleep suddenly seemed ridiculous. Slowly the tension collapsed into fatigue. Tears rolled uncontrollably down my sweaty face, which was set in an idiot's grin.

'Feel any better?' said Alcyone quietly from the doorway of the engineering room.

'Terrible, and ridiculously stupid. How could I ever let myself get into this state?' I said wiping away the tears with my sleeve.

'It happens to us all from time to time. We call it space sickness.'

'Whatever it is, it's quite shattering.'

'That's right. Space sickness seems to be an all-mental struggle with one's inner self,' said Alcyone helping me to my feet.

'You mean you felt like this when we left Earth?'

'Something like it.'

It was the way Alcyone replied that gave me a new sense of uneasiness. We took the lift all the way to the flight deck, where Betelgeuse was on duty.

'One game I learned on Earth which gives me great satisfaction,' said Betelgeuse as we stepped from the lift.

'Chess is a good mental exercise,' I managed to say, seeing the board set up on the console.

Something was prodding the back of my mind. A feeling, a strange suspicion. 'Why did we all get space sickness?' I asked at length.

'What?' exclaimed Betelgeuse, in some surprise.

'I was telling Dick about space sickness,' said Alcyone.

'Come on. I'm not simple-minded. Just what *has* been going on?'

'What do you mean?' asked Betelgeuse. 'Everything seems to be going well. Alcyone, what is this space sickness you're talking about?'

'Betelgeuse . . .' I started.

Alcyone put her finger to her lip, indicating to me to be

quiet. Something was still wrong. Through my weariness I struggled to formulate a picture of what was happening but nothing suggested itself. I glanced again at Betelgeuse, who smiled fixedly as he continued his game of solitary chess. Alcyone looked in my direction and then quietly left the flight deck.

Now that I was coming more or less back to my usual state of mind I began to realize that whatever this space sickness was, it hadn't produced the same symptoms in all of us. This I felt to be distinctly odd. There was something peculiar about it, something far from normal.

The computer bleeped. Betelgeuse read the printout and then frantically typed a series of instructions.

'Unidentified object 10 degrees to starboard,' he called out, apparently returning to his fully alert mental state.

'There it is,' he exclaimed a moment later, pointing to a bright spot on the radar scan.

'What can I do?' I asked, moving over to the flight console.

'Just sit tight. I've sent a coded message to see if it's one of ours.'

'How long does it take for a reply?'

'Not long. The computer in any of our ships is programmed to reply automatically to this particular message.'

'If no reply?'

'Then the object is alien.'

Rigel, appearing at this moment, went quickly to his post by the computer.

'Negative to our signal,' he said, as the computer divulged its information.

'Withdraw navigational instruments and arm AM torpedoes.'

'There's no chance that it is from the Earth fleet?' I asked.

'We are outrunning the Earth fleet,' answered Rigel.

We all watched the radar scan. The object appeared to

be almost on the same course as we were but a few tens of thousands of kilometres to one side. Slowly we started to reduce the distance.

'How long before we make contact?' asked Betelgeuse.

'On present nearly parallel courses, 18 hours and 26 minutes,' Rigel replied, 'but very much less than that if we were to make even a small course change.'

'We'll continue present course. Program for immediate retaliation in case of attack.'

'Are you expecting an attack?' I asked, somewhat innocently.

'It could be only a lump of debris. But if it is an alien ship it will attack as soon as the distance between us is reduced to a few kilometres,' Rigel answered.

Before long it became clear that the object was indeed a spacecraft. Betelgeuse attempted again to communicate with it but without result.

'I'd love to have a better sight of that ship,' he said, switching on the optical monitors. 'One day we must devise a better system, one that gives us greater depth of vision,' he added.

The optical screen showed nothing but space and stars, and yet thousands of kilometres away, somewhere out in front of us, was an alien craft.

'There's something I don't understand,' I said. 'How did an alien ship come to be on the same course as ourselves?'

'Find our ships,' Betelgeuse muttered.

'I don't understand either,' said Alcyone, as she returned to the flight deck.

'It seems very strange that your fleet would have left an alien ship intact,' I went on, 'lying in wait for us.'

'Our ships would have taken it in tow,' agreed Rigel thoughtfully.

The computer bleeped and we all moved towards the printout.

'Communications malfunction!' shouted Betelgeuse in total surprise. 'Check all internal systems.'

Rigel hurried about the flight deck. Moments later he shook his head, saying, 'Still registering as a malfunction. I suspect it is something outside the ship that is causing it. All stimulated emission systems are inactive.'

'Microwave amplification dead,' muttered an extremely puzzled Betelgeuse.

I again switched on the outside visual monitors, hoping that as we closed with the alien craft I might be able to see it in some detail.

'We're getting much nearer to that ship,' I said after watching for a while. 'Is there any way we can test for outside jamming of the communication system?'

'That's been done. The only reply to the question is a total communication malfunction,' Rigel answered.

'I don't like this,' grunted Betelgeuse, reading from more printout. 'That ship out there is closing deliberately on to our course.'

'It begins to look as though whoever they are they've been expecting us,' I remarked.

'How could anyone have known?' asked Alcyone.

Betelgeuse was impatient. 'Well, we did blurt out our course on an open signal, didn't we? I should have known that a ship might lie in wait for us.'

'It could also suggest that the bulk of your fleet is running into an ambush.'

'That also had crossed my mind.'

'Eight hundred kilometres, and closingg,' reported Rigel.

'The object is starting to take on a shape,' I reported as a dark form grew slowly on the vision screen.

'Five hundred kilometres,' called Rigel.

'Is our energy output constant?'

'There's been no change since going over to ION power.'

'One hundred kilometres,' reported Alcyone.

'This is very strange,' exclaimed Rigel. 'We have no reading of motive power from that ship. Yet it has changed course in order to close with us.'

'Lights,' commanded Betelgeuse.

A battery of external lights flashed on, immediately revealing a shimmering sphere.

'What the devil . . . ,' I muttered, as we all stared in bewilderment at the strange craft floating alongside us.

'How big is it?' asked Alcyone, being the first to react rationally.

'About a thousand metres across,' I answered.

'Still no sign of motive power?' asked Betelgeuse.

'None.'

'Try communication channels. I've never seen a ship like that before.'

Suddenly the whole inside of our ship was filled with frenzied electronic chatter. We stared at each other for what seemed an eternity, stunned by what we were hearing. The electronic babble now all around us came from the Yela spaceship which hung there in our searchlights like an enormous metallic orange.

6　The Crippled Yela

'Turn that noise off,' cried Betelgeuse in an agonized voice.

By now I understood that to Betelgeuse and his people the electronic chatter had come to be regarded as a kind of death summons.

'It's eerie to get this close to an enemy we have been fighting for so long,' whispered Alcyone, watching the shimmering sphere the whole time.

Rigel managed to cut off the electronic chatter, and we all returned to the vision monitor.

'That ship is disabled,' exclaimed Betelgeuse suddenly.

'Partially disabled, I think,' corrected Rigel. 'Remember that it managed to edge over into our course.'

'If it was fully functional we'd be gone by now,' returned Betelgeuse, typing instructions to the computer, his confidence returned.

'What are you doing?' asked Alcyone.

'I want that ship. We'll see whether a magnetic probe will attach itself to the hull.'

The small probe shot from the side of our ship with its light hawser trailing behind it.

'Probe made contact but no magnetic attraction,' reported Rigel.

'It's possible there may be some point of attachment to which we can actually tie the hawser,' I suggested, becoming interested in the salvage operation.

'Could be, but it will take a long time to search by remote control over so large a sphere,' was Rigel's doubtful comment.

'Then I'll volunteer to go and have a look.'

'Ridiculous,' snorted Betelgeuse.

'Out of the question,' said Alcyone.

'If you want to salvage that ship then stop arguing. Get another probe and a lifeline ready.' I took a space suit from the lockers. 'I'll ride across on the probe and take a quick look over the ship using a jet pack. You'll have to give me a continuous running lifeline so that I'm not dragged away from the sphere until the last moment.'

'We can program a probe to stop just short of the sphere,' answered Rigel, still doubtfully.

I put my space suit on, slung the life-support system over my shoulders, and screwed up all the relevant connections. Alcyone walked quickly round me a couple of times checking that all was well. Finally I switched on my communication system and headed for the lift.

'We'll give you exactly one hour before we start hauling you back here,' crackled Betelgeuse's voice in my headphones.

'O.K.' I stepped from the lift and entered the external airlock. I breathed hard a couple of times to satisfy myself that oxygen was flowing.

'Depressurize.' A cold sweat broke out all over my body. I was regretting now my extreme rashness in volunteering for what could easily prove a lethal expedition. The others had let me go not because they were confident in my ability to do the job but because it was a rigorous rule of their space code that such an offer as mine must never be refused.

I was weightless now. Slowly I floated towards the ceiling of the airlock. Grabbing a support handle I manoeuvred my way along the wall to where the jet packs were housed. A few moments' struggle with the apparatus and then I was ready. 'All set,' I said with more assurance than I felt.

The outer door slowly opened. A squirt with the jet pack sent me careering outside. There was no time to lose as I crudely directed myself toward the probe.

It was a neat device consisting of a small rocket with a

cylindrical head containing additional fuel, a few tools and a reserve life-support system.

'You're on your way,' I heard Betelgeuse say. Then I felt myself being propelled with considerable force towards the silent shimmering sphere. The journey was completed in under five minutes. It was strange to see all the luminous expelled material from the probe's rocket engine and not to hear any sound.

'I'm starting my reconnaissance now,' I reported, releasing the probe. 'The outside of this hull is remarkably smooth, as well as being dazzlingly bright.'

It was difficult to examine the surface of the sphere and to propel myself properly at the same time.

'Sorry about the acrobatics,' I mumbled, slowly coming the right way up. 'The metal surface appears to have been badly burnt. There are scorch marks running ten to twenty metres round the hull. It also looks as if a number of external fittings have been blown off the surface. The whole appearance of the outside is one of being hit by some form of explosion,' I said as I made my way round the sphere.

'Any sign of a door or portholes?' asked Betelgeuse.

'Not so far.' I propelled myself back to the probe.

It was obviously going to take more time than I had available to cover the whole of the exterior. Back at the probe I hunted through the tool box until I found a pressure drill and a large metal plate.

'I'm going to attach a repair plate to the hull and the magnetic probe to that,' I announced.

I picked up the drill and plate and began my task. With the plate pressed firmly against the hull of the sphere, I pressed the drill against each corner in turn, squeezing the trigger each time. Within minutes I had a silvery metallic patch three feet square fixed securely to the golden surface of the Yela ship. All I had to do now was to attach magnetically the probe from our own ship. The work seemed to go easily and quickly so that I was surprised to hear Betelgeuse say, 'Only eight minutes to zero, Dick.'

The searchlights in which I was working were extinguished without warning. I foolishly stared towards the home ship and was momentarily blinded when the lights came on again two or three minutes later.

Gropingly I stowed the tools away. Then as my dark adaptation returned, I attached myself to the metallic hawser, which now connected the two ships, using a free-running carabiner. Gradually, my lifeline became taut as Betelgeuse took up the slack, and I started to glide back to our ship.

Inside the airlock I waited for pressurization. Only then did it occur to me how easy it had all been. For a brief moment I wondered if it hadn't been too easy – and then dismissed the thought. Out of the weightless airlock and into the ship, I received congratulations with such modesty as I could muster, and said, 'There was just nothing to be seen out there, except a perfectly smooth sphere. Did you see anything from here?'

'Nothing, nothing at all,' answered Alcyone. 'The sphere just floated there while you made the attachment.'

'The Yela is a total malfunction,' said Betelgeuse, well pleased with himself.

'What happened to the ship's lights?' I asked, getting rid of my suit.

'They suddenly fused. No apparent reason, just an electrical overload.'

'The more I consider the situation,' I went on, 'the more I suspect the sphere out there to be internally intact. But externally it has lost its eyes and ears.'

'Blind. I can understand that. The creature is blind,' exclaimed Rigel.

'Inside that metallic sphere are all the life-support systems needed to keep the Yela alive,' I continued.

'When you were looking at the outside, Dick, you said you didn't see any openings or hatches,' said Alcyone.

'No, it all seemed completely sealed up. Somehow the creature has lost its external sensors. They seem to have been blasted away – by some kind of external explosion.'

'What about motive power?' asked Rigel.

'I couldn't see any engine.'

'Which checks with our failure to detect evidence of jet emission.'

'Incredible,' said Alcyone looking at the sphere, still hanging there, vast and golden.

'It could be a huge robot, a single gigantic computer,' I suggested.

I looked up at the vision screen and wondered just what we would eventually find inside the shimmering golden image. Something caught my eye.

'Look there,' I said, pointing to the shiny metal cylinder.

'It's one of our telescopes,' Rigel exclaimed.

'One of our telescopes,' repeated Betelgeuse in disbelief.

'Yes.'

'Did you give instructions for them to be launched?'

'No, but I thought you had.'

'Quite certainly I did not. I remember distinctly giving instructions for all navigational instruments to be withdrawn,' stated Betelgeuse. He gave the computer a series of commands. We all waited in silence, but no bleep was forthcoming to signal an answer.

'Another malfunction,' growled Betelgeuse, tapping the console with his fingers.

'I'll get the service manual,' said Rigel vanishing into the lift.

'We've never had a total breakdown before. At least not that I can remember,' Alcyone remarked thoughtfully.

'I was under the impression that all your hardware was fitted with self-correction procedures.'

'It is. I was just trying to remember whether I'd given the computer some incorrect source language,' replied Betelgeuse.

'Whatever is wrong, it seems odd that there hasn't been a bleep from the machine telling us of the malfunction,' he went on in a thoroughly puzzled tone.

'Here are all the debugging programs,' cried Rigel, hurrying from the lift with an armful of manuals.

'Is there anything in those manuals about the cutting off of complete computer control?' asked Betelgeuse, taking up an electronic pen and a hand calculator.

'Are you implying that the computer has taken over the running of the ship?' I asked in astonishment.

'It may sound ridiculous, but until I can get the computer to respond to simple instructions I can't cut off its own power supply. Once I can do that, we go automatically on to manual control,' said Betelgeuse, avoiding my question.

'Why can't the power be cut at source?'

'Because we would then have a total shutdown on all the ship's systems, not just the computer. But let's try the usual debugging procedure. It that doesn't work then more drastic measures will have to be taken.' As he turned to the computer, I could see that he was sweating freely.

'It's getting very hot,' he murmured and slumped into his chair. I put my hand to my face. I could feel beads of perspiration falling off my nose.

'The life-support system!' cried Alcyone urgently. 'The computer must be bypassed, otherwise we're dead. Rigel, Dick, get the portable life-support systems ready.'

I began to feel faint, for the temperature had started to rise almost instantaneously, as if we had suddenly become exposed to some vast furnace. I was vaguely aware that Betelgeuse had slumped to the floor. Somehow Rigel managed to carry the life-support systems and helmets from their locker into the middle of the room. Clumsily I stumbled over to where Betelgeuse lay, placed a helmet over his head and turned a support system on.

'It's the best we can do till he comes round,' I gasped, pushing a suit in the direction of Alcyone.

The effort involved in getting into the suits was almost more than we could manage, for in addition to the soaring temperature the oxygen level was now falling catastrophically. Alcyone slumped exhausted half in her suit while Rigel just stood there motionless. The world before my eyes was fast going grey. With what I knew to be a last effort I managed to get inside a suit with the support system turned on.

After what seemed an age, actually less than three minutes, the world returned to normal shape. I now found it easy to close my helmet. Moving over to where Alcyone lay, I turned on the oxygen in her helmet. Then I crawled to Rigel and more or less stuffed him into his suit, noticing that he was turning a strange shade of blue.

'Is he all right?' I said, breathing hard as Alcyone crawled to my side. Alcyone took no notice of my question. I switched on her headset and repeated my inquiry.

'I think so,' she said hoarsely.

Betelgeuse seemed to be coming round and struggling to remove his helmet. It took a great amount of severe physical restraint to fix him firmly in his suit.

'God, that was a close call,' I groaned, sitting down on a seat.

'Dick,' Alcyone said urgently, 'the main support system must be started at once. These packs won't last for very long.'

'Then come on, Rigel. Let's begin by cutting the power to that damned computer.' I took his arm and guided him into the lift.

'The main control box is in the engineering room,' he managed to gasp before becoming unconscious again.

The engineering room was on the very bottom level. Once inside I looked at the banks of instruments that lined three of the walls. There was little to show on any of them. On the fourth wall was a vast workbench carrying an array of engineering tools and equipment. I heaved the semiconscious Rigel to the bench and propped him up.

'Over there,' he said, pointing feebly.

The electronic switchboard was alive with flashing indicators and lighted switches. I found the computer power switch and opened it. All lights went out immediately.

'The next switch on your right, press it down,' came Rigel's voice through my earpieces. I pressed and the lights slowly came up again. I took a hard look at the switchboard and then proceeded to press all the buttons marked 'manual'. To my surprise the instruments on the three walls came alive again.

'Life support is very critical,' Rigel croaked.

'It must be functioning now.' I pressed the manual buttons a second time to make certain.

'The system is above critical level, but only enough to support us in an exhausted state.'

It was at that moment, watching Rigel swaying helplessly on the bench, that I realized what was happening to the ship. A shiver ran through my body. Sweat drenched my face. For I now understood that, in addition to the four of us, a fifth intelligence was aboard the ship. The Yela was also here.

7 Fight for Survival

'We've got to get rid of it,' I said quietly to Rigel.

'I had come to the same conclusion, but we shall have to work quickly.' He stared bleakly at the instruments covering the walls of the engineering room.

'What usually happens when there is a malfunction in the main life-support system?'

'If it were irreparable, we'd try to build another one. But such a disaster has never happened in my experience.'

'Well, that's what we must try to do now.'

'We could dismantle the whole system and attempt to rebuild it,' suggested Rigel.

'I doubt if that would be a good idea.'

'Why not?'

'Because we must work near to these manual controls,' I said, indicating the switches on the walls. 'Otherwise we're at the mercy of the computer.'

'Which means the Yela?'

'Yes.'

'If we built a new unit in here, what would happen to the main one?'

'We could use it to recharge these packs,' I said, pointing over my shoulder.

'That makes good sense,' Rigel nodded. 'I'll get started right away.'

When I regained the flight deck, Betelgeuse was stretched out over his seat, while Alcyone was staring glumly around the galley.

'What's wrong?' I asked.

'The computer let the temperature rise in all these synthetic food containers. It has ruined several months' supply of good food.'

'Would it be possible to take all the food-synthesizing equipment down to the engineering room?'

'I suppose so, but why?'

'The only control we have now is manual, which means we must work from the engineering shop .The flight deck here is useless to us, because we are no longer in control of the computer.'

'That is good sense, but what are we going to do about him?' she asked, pointing to the dark sphere on the vision screen.

'When we're installed in the engineering room, we'll give him the chop. Cut the hawser.'

'That could be very dangerous. There is a big tension now in the hawser. It would whip very violently if it were cut.'

'It would be no more dangerous than the present situation. How's Betelgeuse?'

'Very weak. Luckily I don't think there is permanent damage.'

'Thank goodness for that. He was without oxygen for quite a while.'

'I'm sure he'll recover,' she said with a conviction that I hoped would not prove misplaced.

'What normally happens if someone is critically hurt?'

'Well, usually there would be a medical ship fairly close at hand. Since there isn't, we must rely on our own diagnosis and treatment.'

'He doesn't look at all healthy.'

'Leave him. We'll get everything ready in the engineering room first and then bring him down.'

'You're sure? Can't you give him a stimulant or something?'

'Come on, we have work to do,' said Alcyone, her former apathy replaced by a new determination.

Rigel had half the floor covered with cylinders, tools, power packs and an array of pipes.

'Betelgeuse?' he asked looking up from his work.

'O.K.,' replied Alcyone. 'Where can I set up the galley?'

'Anywhere you like,' I said, watching her walk round the room examining the instruments.

'It doesn't look very good,' she said, shaking her head.

'Is there a cutting tool?' I asked Rigel.

He handed me a small pistol-shaped torch with two cylinders attached to it. 'Pull the trigger, it's self-igniting.'

'Right. I'll see what I can do to cut ourselves free of the Yela ship.'

'You'll find the airlock-operating switches inside a small panel near the exit door,' Rigel informed me as I left the room.

Releasing the airlock, I managed without difficulty to open the inner door. It took a moment to get into a jet pack. Then I was ready. Pressing a button closed the inner door. After a final check on my equipment I decompressed the interior of the airlock and then operated the outer-door release switch. Nothing happened. There I was, holding on to the grab rail in a weightless condition, punching as hard as I could on the release switch. Still the door remained closed.

'Damn it, Rigel,' I muttered into the microphone in my helmet, 'the blasted outer door won't open.'

All I heard in reply was the thumping of my own heart. After a last desperate push on the switch, again without result, I activated the recompression circuit. To my intense relief I stopped floating. My feet came slowly to the air-lock floor. I took the jet pack off and pressed the inner-door release switch. Nothing happened. In the fury that was welling up inside me I literally punched the switch, but again with zero results.

'Hello, can anyone hear me?' I shouted, 'I'm stuck in the airlock.' Again there was no reply. In this ridiculous predicament there seemed but one thing I could do. I pressed the nozzle of the cutting torch against the inner door and pulled the trigger. There was a shower of sparks and a small neat hole appeared.

Two to three minutes later I was clambering through an enlarged hole. In the corridor again I pressed the inner-door release switch, once more with negative result.

'Dick,' cried Alcyone in surprise when I returned to the engineering room, 'what happened?'

'The damned doors in the airlock jammed.'

'Did you cut the hawser?' Rigel asked anxiously.

'No, I did not. The outer door wouldn't open. When I tried to come back, the blasted inner door jammed too.'

'There's nothing apparently wrong with that part of the electrical system,' grunted Rigel, peering at the various monitoring devices.

Suddenly the ship gave a terrific lurch. I was thrown off balance and landed hard on my back.

'What the hell was that?' muttered Alcyone, clinging to a food container.

'A change of the pressure compensation,' I suggested.

'No, that wasn't a change of pressure. It was an impulsive change in the motion of the ship itself,' stated Rigel.

'We must free ourselves, Dick,' he continued.

'Too true, but how?'

'I think the best way would be to remove the whole of the probe housing. It's secured in a small tube above number 4 torpedo tube.'

'How small is the tube?'

'About a meter in diameter.'

'I can crawl down it, then?'

'Yes, but the probe is mounted to a plate which blocks the tube off from the space outside.'

'So what can we do?'

'Well,' he said operating a switch, 'we must begin by building an airlock within the tube itself.'

'Is the mechanism for opening the tube on the same circuitry as the airlock door?'

'No.'

'Can it be closed manually?'

'Yes.'

The ship lurched violently again. This time there was an accompanying increase in the drive pressure.

'Better check course,' I gasped. Rigel staggered to a boxlike object which he had rigged up as a small console.

'It won't be very accurate, because I have to use visual readings.'

Suddenly he turned in amazement. 'We're 15 degrees or thereabouts off course, in a direction towards Ursa Major,' he exclaimed in a hoarse voice.

By clicking various switches we managed to get the screen lit up on the little console. It showed the dark silhouette of the Yela sphere. Then Rigel moved the scan until it picked up the constellation of Centaurus. Something was wrong here, dreadfully wrong.

'Go back again to the sphere,' I yelled.

Alcyone, Rigel and I gathered close to the tiny box. 'See,' I went on excitedly, 'the sphere is *ahead* of us. We're not towing it. *The damn thing is towing us.*'

'So that's why we lurched around so badly!' exclaimed Rigel.

He stood there, staring fixedly at me. We were helpless, not just within our own ship. We had even lost control over our destination. We were headed now for Ursa Major, for the territory of the Yela.

'I don't understand it,' muttered Alcyone.

'I'm afraid I understand it all too well,' I began grimly. 'The Yela was crippled only in the sense that it had an urgent need for primary power. Now it has taken over the power from our generators.'

'Through the hawser!'

'Yes, through the hawser. Now it can operate all its own internal systems.'

'Including the main drive,' nodded Rigel, gazing again at the monitor. For a while we all silently watched the sphere ahead of us. Then Rigel consulted an intricate bank of electrical instruments.

'We are now getting a very strong indication of motive power from the Yela ship,' he announced.

'Are you saying the Yela actually lay in wait for us?' asked Alcyone in an astonished tone.

'I'm saying very much more than that. I'm saying the Yela can somehow read our thoughts, and that it somehow exercised a kind of hypnotic control over us.'

'Hypnotic control!'

'Remember how strange we all felt? I find myself wondering if your main fleet was ever on the course it was supposed to be on.'

'You mean we were put on to that course by the Yela?'

'Yes, that's what I mean. How else would we just happen to pass close by a crippled ship?'

There was a deep rumbling in Rigel's throat. 'I do not understand why we did not have suspicions,' he growled.

'*Why* did we attach the probe?'

'A kind of euphoria.'

'From the Yela?'

'Yes, from the Yela.'

'You said the Yela can read our thoughts!' interrupted Alcyone.

'From the electrical signals in our intercommunication system. That was why the main life-support system was cut, to force us into these suits, to force us to use electrical communication, instead of ordinary sound in the air.'

'You mean the Yela cannot detect ordinary sound waves?'

'Not unless a microphone were alive somewhere.'

'So that is how the Yela knew you were going to try to cut the hawser!' exclaimed Alcyone.

'Yes, it knew minutes in advance.'

'So it instructed the computer to trap you in the air-lock.'

'Right. That's exactly what happened.'

We all became silent for a moment. Then Rigel said, 'And it can read our thoughts now!'

'It can, until we screen this room completely. We need to do that, as well as to build our own life-support system,' I concluded.

The following hundreds of hours were both awkward and painful. We started writing down our important conversations to make certain the Yela couldn't interpret our thoughts. Fortunately, Betelgeuse returned at last to normal health. We set about the construction of our auxiliary life-support system. But knowing we were doing this, the Yela cut the main system to an absolutely critical level, wishing to keep us alive, it seemed, but only barely so – perhaps as an insurance, in case we might be needed again, as I had been needed in my space walk to fix the probe.

By reducing our needs to the barest minimum we just managed to recharge two support packs every eight hours. Betelgeuse and I would work, using support packs, and then turn things over to Alcyone and Rigel. While they laboriously constructed the unit, we would lie on the floor gasping for breath. In case of emergency, we kept four packs, fully charged, close at hand.

Apart from the suffocating lack of oxygen, we also had to contend with a progressive fall of temperature. This was hardly noticeable at first. Normally, the temperature was run at a constant 20 degrees centigrade. After the first fifty hours the thermometer was found to be at 19.5 degrees centigrade. Another fifty hours later the temperature had dropped another half a degree. So it went on. It became obvious that the heating part of the life-support system was also being tampered with by the Yela. Rigel eventually set about constructing a manually operated generator, which we kept in reserve along with the additional support packs and some fuel cells.

In the thin air it was remarkable how even a small drop in temperature was easily and quickly noticeable. The time spent without oxygen from the packs became more and more of an ordeal. I found myself laughing repeatedly for no reason. These bouts of hysteria became more and more difficult to control.

As the temperature dropped it became easier to sleep during the off-work periods. It also became increasingly more difficult to wake each other after the rest periods. To me death had never been a major source of interest or conflict. I knew that sooner or later my body functions would cease and I would be declared dead. But the very strangeness of our present predicament appeared to heighten my fear of death. It was remarkable to me how perfectly calm the others were. They simply accepted that the Yela was a superior creature and that it would end our lives when it was ready to do so. There was little fury or fight in them. They worked on because I worked on, determined as I was to see the Yela in hell for it. But enthusiasm can be contagious. My will to live seemed to help the others and in the end they contributed as much as or more than I did to our eventual safety. In sum, then, the life-support system was completed, and we began at last to breathe more easily.

Fortunately the power required to run the system was fairly small and could be handled by the self-contained generating plant, which Rigel managed by deft engineering to adapt to our needs.

After collecting all the equipment we felt we might need, which included all available manuals, we set about screening the room and sealing the outer door of the engineering room. Then with the life-support system running well we turned to our next problem, the desperate need for a source of heat. Rigel soon produced an electric fire, which he attempted to work off the still-functioning lighting circuit. Unfortunately our needs turned out to be far in excess of the power available in the circuit.

Alcyone kept a good supply of food going, which enabled us to shrug off the chill for a time, but eventually the cold consumed our attention. Sleep became an evil. At $T+4,300$, some 2,000 hours after we should have met up with the main body of Betelgeuse's fleet, the temperature inside the engineering room had sunk to forty degrees below zero. Except when we needed to be momentarily free to carry out some critical manual operation, we were obliged now to remain in our space suits. So once again we had been forced from natural sound communication to electrical communication. Unless our hastily erected screen was being fully effective, the Yela could once again read any messages we might interchange on our intercom system.

Our surroundings looked more like the inside of a deep freeze than a machine shop. The walls, floors, even the tools were all covered with a thin coating of white ice crystals. It was now of the utmost importance to keep the generator working in order that the life-support system would continue to function. We took turns winding laboriously at the thing for half an hour at a time, while the others huddled together trying to keep warm.

It was about at this stage that Rigel noticed a red light gleaming beneath the crystals on the small console. Clearing the ice away, we saw from the monitors that the ship's main life-support system had ceased entirely to function, from which I concluded that the Yela had at last decided to have done with us.

The temperature continued to fall. At last the monitoring instruments ceased to function altogether. For Betelgeuse, this was indeed the end of the road. He was now the captain of an entirely blind ship, a ship whose motion was wholly out of his control. At this desperate stage he agreed at last to a dangerous course, one that I would have taken myself long ago: namely, to fire a little of the ship's remaining chemical fuel. It had been against all his instincts and experience to permit a naked flame to be exposed within the ship, but now in the end this is what it had come down to.

The first step was to collect a jet pack from a store close by the airlock. After unsealing the shop door, I set off to make the journey to the outer skin of the ship. It seemed like making my way through a great frozen cavern, the walls and floor glittering with a profusion of ice crystals.

I secured a jet pack and returned to the engineering room without serious incident. It was proposed to use the small rocket motor to create our open flame. Since there was only a very limited fuel supply in the pack itself, Rigel and Betelgeuse went off to assess the situation at the main fuel tanks. After a while Betelgeuse returned with the unpleasant news that the ION engine had ceased to function. A few moments later Rigel came with the more cheerful information that he had found a possible tapping point, to which I was then instructed to lay a small-diameter pipe.

At first all seemed to go splendidly, but the cold steadily consumed our energy. We were forced repeatedly to put on our insulated suits and to eat as much synthetic food as we could masticate. The heavy suits greatly impeded the speed with which we could tackle the more delicate parts of the work.

Betelgeuse stripped the jet pack and secured the motor to the workbench, which we proposed to use as a kind of testbed. Finally all the pipe connections were made and tested as best we could. The critical moment had come. Rigel turned on the fuel supply. There was a slight hiss as the hydrogen–oxygen mixture flowed over the burner catalyst. Then with a sharp crackling explosion the gas ignited. A jet of flame jumped high into the room. Quickly we limited the fuel flow until the flame was reduced to a more reasonable length. Then we sat back, praying there would be no serious leak in our improvised system.

As the hours went by the temperature rose. The apparently never-ending pain in our bones began to recede. We were even able to eat defrosted food. It seemed a greater luxury than anything I could remember from my life on the Earth.

A new-found enthusiasm began to well up in all of us. We talked – using natural sound – of ways to escape the control of the Yela. Rigel suggested we should repair the damaged airlock door and then make a further attempt to open the outer door of the ship. Since the vision monitors still were not working, this would at least permit us to determine our present flight path. The idea met with general approval and we set immediately about the repair job.

Since no power was available in the rest of the ship, it was necessary to remove the airlock door by hand, and then to carry it to the engineering shop, where we still had our precious store of fuel cells. Rigel set up a kind of small knitting machine. The fuel cells managed to work it, but only sluggishly. It moved slowly backwards and forwards across the hole, and in the last moment of the operation the machine laboured under a nearly exhausted power supply.

Refitting the door took much longer than the dismantling. Once it was in place we were able to test manoeuvrability by winding it backwards and forwards on a rack-and-pinion system located above the door support. The difficulties in this phase of the operation were compounded by the need to wear our space suits and by our determination to use the intercom system as little as possible.

Betelgeuse and Rigel used a hand pump to depressurize the airlock, while Alcyone and I worked determinedly on the opening mechanism to the external door. It seemed like trying to lift a very heavy car with a very small jack. But at length I could see the door moving centimetre by centimetre.

Betelgeuse came through the airlock and attached us both to lifelines. Depressurization and weightlessness followed. We worked on with aching muscles, for we had to brace our bodies to prevent ourselves from floating round and round the handle while we turned it.

At length we had the door open just enough for me to poke my helmet through. I could feel the adrenaline heighten my senses. I put up my hand to the edge of the door in order to steady myself. Then I eased my head through the gap and looked around.

'It's black, as black as hell,' I said in a hoarse whisper.

8   At the Edge of Oblivion

In amazement and shock I withdrew awkwardly from the partly open airlock door. The gap was so narrow and my space suit so bulky that I had real difficulty, leading to a moment of panic, in getting my head and shoulders back through the gap.

'What is it?' whispered Alcyone.

'I don't know. Better take a look yourself,' I suggested.

Alcyone moved past me and was just on the point of working her way around the side of the door when Betelgeuse's voice crackled violently in my ear, 'Get back here quick. There is now a total malfunction.'

While Alcyone rejoined me I wondered what kind of malfunction could be any more total than the one we'd been experiencing for the last few thousand hours. It seemed to take forever to get the outer door closed, and all the time Betelgeuse kept urging us to return through the inner door.

'We've done it. We've got it closed,' I panted at last.

'Then we will open the inner door and pull you through with the lifelines.'

'How about depressurizing?'

'There is *no* pressure,' came the ominous reply.

A few moments later we were back with Betelgeuse and Rigel, for it was easy for them to haul us on the lifelines, since we were weightless. We were weightless now within the ship as well as within the airlock.

'The drive has gone,' explained Rigel.

'You mean the Yela has lost its motive power?' I asked.

'That's the way it looks. Since our ION engine ceased to operate the Yela has lost its source of primary power.'

'We have no time to lose,' broke in Betelgeuse. 'The situation is critically dangerous.'

'Why?'

'Because of leaks in our improvised fuel system. Under weightless conditions leaks may develop.'

I saw now what should have been obvious before. Under weightlessness all the stress relationships in our makeshift arrangements in the engineering shop would be changed. A leak of the highly unstable hydrogen–oxygen mixture, with the gas gradually spreading, would be only too likely to lead to explosion and to a total disintegration of the whole ship.

'We must turn off the fuel supply,' I said.

'At the main tank, Dick,' agreed Betelgeuse. 'You made the connection there. Now you'd better go back and dismantle your fuel-supply system. The rest of us will make our way back to the engineering shop. Meet us there.'

We set off on our respective journeys. If the ice-coated interior of the ship had seemed spectacular before, the situation had now become totally fantastic. Before, we had experienced more or less normal pressure conditions. We had been able to walk and to climb, albeit in our space suits, through the vast icy cavern of the ship. Now I had to swim weightless from corridor to corridor, from deck to deck. On my previous journey to the main fuel tank it had not worried me unduly that for part of the time I was entirely cut off from the others, for in the region of the fuel tanks the electronic repeaters, which normally permitted the intercom system to function all over the ship, were unserviceable – presumably because of the great fall in temperature. But now, on my second journey, the sense of isolation was far greater. In fact, as I floated along, my only sensory input came from the things I could see. I came at last to Y corridor, between the second and third decks, and it was there that the ship's lights went out. In total blackness, I was now without real sensation, for the space suit prevented me from gaining any sensitive awareness of my surroundings. I hung suspended, weightless, without sight, smell or sound, and very nearly without touch. Under such conditions a man quickly becomes a vegetable.

I called in desperation on the intercom system, but there was still no reply. Then I went on talking, since the sound of my own voice was a tiny island of sensation in the vast seas of oblivion that now surrounded me. If Rigel was right, both the Yela ship and our own were entirely without power. If only our party were not split, this would be an opportunity to cut the hawser, for the Yela could take no action now against us. We would need to operate the airlock manually, of course, but then we had just proved this to be feasible. The space walk would be exceedingly hazardous, but then there was nothing in principle to stop us from trying. With the hawser cut we might be able to get at least some of the ship's systems back to normal functioning. And if we could restart the ION engine, all would not be lost.

Even as I formulated the plan I knew it to be hopeless. Without light and without first making careful preparations it would be hopeless. It would even be well-nigh hopeless for me to find my companions. All I could do would be to move about the ship at random, on the chance that I might reach some place where the intercom repeaters were working. Then I realized that with the loss of power it was likely that none of the repeaters would be working anywhere in the ship.

'How can you get so stupid!' I exclaimed. I had suddenly realized that the Yela might well be still able to pick up the electrical signals from my intercom transmitter, which was still being activated from batteries carried in the back pocket of my space suit. Yet what did it matter? The Yela was as helpless as we were – or nearly so. With this thought the vague beginnings of a plan occurred to me.

'You're nothing but a big stupid oaf,' I said, talking

quite intentionally now to the Yela. 'You're just as finished as we are, except that death will be a lot easier for us. You're going to linger on for a long time yet, with nothing to do except to think about your mistakes. While our engines were operative you had access to primary power. You had everything going for you. But then, just to deal with four puny humans, you interfered with our controls, to the point where a low-temperature fault has developed in our main system. Through your stupidity you've now destroyed yourself.'

I paused for a moment, wondering what the Yela would make of these insults. It was possible that during the period of access to our power supply the creature had managed to send out messages to others of its kind, and that it might eventually receive assistance in some way. Although this was possible, I doubted it. This particular creature was almost blind. It had lost its external sensors and consequently would not have been able to send out much in the way of an SOS. Conceivably, it might have used the transmission system in our own ship. If so, how much faith would it have in the efficiency of our system? Not too much, I hoped. It was essential for the Yela to be thoroughly disturbed about its predicament.

'I am not in the least afraid of you. In fact I am the chap who drove you back with the solar lithium bomb,' I went on, speaking boastfully into the intercom mike. I waited, floating in the darkness, wondering if the Yela could be receiving my transmission. Was the Yela entirely out of power? Surely not. The creature must have a reserve of some kind, just as we carried storage batteries as a reserve. Then an oddly disturbing thought occurred to me. Perhaps the Yela was dead already. As if to dispel the thought, there came a burst of electronic chatter on my headset. I turned the gain control to its lowest point to avoid the deafening violence of it. Although I had no understanding of meaning, I sensed a hysterical quality in the Yela's response. Possibly it had been the solar outburst, triggered by the lithium bomb, which had half-fried the creature, which had caused the scorch marks I had seen on the shimmering sphere, and which had stripped away its sensory perceptors.

'There is no possibility of any of us surviving,' I continued, 'unless the engines of this ship are restarted. Since this can no longer be done through automatic control, the only possibility is manual. And that means *us*. We need vital parts of the ship's system to be unthawed. We need the automatic controls, which are now locked, to become unlocked. All this needs power, which *you* must supply from your reserve. The flow of power along the connecting hawser must be reversed. First you must reactivate the lighting circuit so that we can collect ourselves together and then make preparations for maintaining our life-support system. Otherwise we are dead – and so are you.'

I floated on and on for what seemed an age, always in darkness. In desperation, I moved now with more vigour than I had done formerly. I turned the gain control on my earpiece to maximum setting, so that there was a quite loud hiss due to amplifier noise. I began to imagine I could hear voices there inside the noise. At first I dismissed the impression of voices as fantasy, but then I tried steering myself from place to place to discover if there was a direction in which I might travel in order to improve their audibility.

My motion carried me straight into some V-shaped obstacle, giving me a good thump and wedging firmly the upper part of my body. The more I struggled to free myself the more tightly did I become fastened. The awkward space suit made effective movement almost impossible. At length I lay there quietly, wondering if the suit were acting like the head of a harpoon, going in easily but never coming out again. I confined myself now to small movements and to light pressures, gradually seeking easier positions. Suddenly everything loosened and I was free once more. Almost immediately after that I heard Betelgeuse's voice in my earpiece. Although the voice was low and faint, I was listening to pure amplifier noise no longer.

'Betelgeuse,' I gasped, 'where are you?'

After a long pause there came his reply. 'Dick, we're down on K deck. Can you make it here?'

'I don't know where I am in the dark.'

'Dark! We've got some light now.'

'Now?'

'Yes, it was off for a while. But we've got enough to see by, although the intensity is very weak.'

'Keep talking,' I instructed, 'so that I can steer on sound volume.'

'You will only find the nearest repeater,' broke in Rigel.

'I don't think the repeaters are working.'

'Then you must be quite close.'

'I hope so. In any case we're in communication again. Which is a big improvement.'

The searching for a path through the ship towards my companions went on with agonizing slowness. The volume of their voices rose and fell with astonishing complexity. There was no obvious route to be chosen. Sometimes the volume would fall for a while before rising to a higher level. At last in the distance I saw a faint radiance. It grew brighter as I swam laboriously through a veritable sea of metallic obstacles. The light eventually became strong enough for me to see ahead, and from there on I moved with much greater precision. Within minutes I re-joined my companions.

'Dick, I couldn't think what might have happened,' exclaimed Alcyone.

'The lights in my part of the ship went out.'

'They did here too.'

'Then they came on again – faintly, as you can see,' added Rigel.

'I don't know what malfunction could have produced that kind of behaviour,' grunted Betelgeuse.

I thought of telling them of my attempt to communicate

with the Yela but decided that any such idea would seem strange and would probably be unwelcome.

'I wasn't able to get as far as the main fuel tank. That part of the ship is in darkness,' I said.

'We've managed to shut off the fuel supply at this end,' Alcyone explained.

'But it would be better at the main tank,' Betelgeuse continued grumpily.

'So what is to be done next?'

'I don't know. I just don't know,' he replied dejectedly.

'Can we use the chemical fuel to start up a standby generator?'

'For what purpose?'

'We could use the power to restart the ION engine and to work the main life-support system.'

'We could try. But in these suits it would be very hard.'

'The ION engine needs very little power. Perhaps there is enough already in the lighting circuit,' suggested Alcyone.

Rigel grunted in disagreement. 'The ION engine has failed because of the low temperature of the components in the control channel. It would be useless to attempt to restart it without first raising the temperature.'

'Which means the main life-support system must come first?'

'Yes. It is a pity the automatic controls are locked against us.'

'Why?'

'Otherwise we might have tried to use the power in the lighting circuit – to activate the temperature control, at least.'

'I don't understand.'

'If we could activate the temperature control, a large standby generator would automatically be brought into operation,' explained Alcyone.

'Where?'

'In the main system.'

'Using the chemical fuel?'

'Yes.'

'Then why is there any difficulty?' I asked.

'Because the controls are locked,' explained Rigel woodenly.

'The controls aren't functioning. Nothing is functioning.'

'They will come on again as soon as the power returns. Everything is programed to revert to the situation as it was before the power went off.'

'Can't it be changed?'

'No. The program is in the computer hardware, I'm afraid,' interposed Betelgeuse. 'It was built that way because it was thought to be safer.'

'Perhaps it won't work like that,' I suggested.

'Why not?'

'Well, everything seems to be a malfunction, doesn't it?'

'It might be worth a try,' Betelgeuse agreed. This was something of a relief to me. I had hopes the Yela might itself change the controls, but I still didn't wish to explain my way of thinking to the others.

'We can try from the engineering shop. It will be something to do,' Betelgeuse concluded.

We swam our way along frost-lined corridors back to the shop again. Rigel began to throw switches and to press buttons as quickly as his space suit would allow. The lights went out again as power was deflected into other circuits. For a moment the light returned, much brighter than before. With the return of an all-embracing blackness we knew the first attempt to fire the main-system standby generator had failed. Rigel continued to work away at a second attempt, while Betelgeuse did what he could to help. Alcyone and I simply wedged ourselves against one of the benches – and waited. I will pass quickly over the anxious hour that followed the first attempt and how Rigel contrived to augment the meagre power in the lighting

... every bit of support he could wring from the
...ge batteries. At last the lights came on and

'...ed standby generator is now operative,' Rigel
announced in an exhausted but satisfied voice.

'Now we must watch the automatic controls,' grunted
Betelgeuse.

We floated there in the engineering shop, moving weight-
lessly along the walls where the switches and monitors
were mounted. We all knew a crisis to be approaching, for
our life-support systems were not far from exhaustion.
There came a cry from Alcyone and we moved as fast as
we could manage toward her. Thinking her support system must have been less completely charged than the
others, I was mightily relieved to hear Betelgeuse shout,

'The temperature is rising!'

'Where?' I gasped. It didn't seem to be rising there in
the engineering shop. Indeed we were all numb with cold
and had been so for many hours.

'On the flight deck,' answered Rigel.

I could see the light appearing on the control board and
needles on various meters had moved away from their zero
points.

'So that part at least of the automatic lock seems to have
been removed?'

'It would appear so,' answered Betelgeuse, still grunting.

'Perhaps we should all go to the flight deck?'

'You and Alcyone go first. Rigel and I still have some
adjustments to make.'

'We need to check on the flow of chemical fuel,' explained Rigel.

With the lights on throughout the ship, there was little
difficulty in reaching the flight deck. I knew Betelgeuse was
still desperately worried about fuel leaks, which could all
too easily make the whole ship unstable. But for myself, I
was worried by the short time remaining before our support packs would cease to function. It was with a profound

sense of relief that we found the temperature to have risen, by nearly seven degrees centigrade. Most crucial of all, oxygen was available at a number of valve points. By the time Betelgeuse and Rigel rejoined us, Alcyone and I had oxygen masks ready for the four of us. We would need to remain in our suits until the temperature rose a great deal more, but with the oxygen masks replacing our life-support packs, which were now close to their last gasp, at least this crisis had been overcome. Unfortunately our faces would be exposed for a time to the bitter cold. I thought it would be ironic if in the end we were all to die of frostbite, so close might we be to a return to tolerable conditions.

However, Rigel had yet another trick up his sleeve. With the power supply from the generator, which was adequate for most ordinary purposes, he arranged to heat a long metallic bar. By standing close by the bar, our masks donned, we managed to combat the icy cold, until after about two hours the temperature had risen suffici-ently for us to remove our suits. And by now, with all exits from the flight deck well sealed, we had a sufficient oxygen content in the air for us to dispense with the masks. At last, after what seemed an uncountable interval of time, we were able to move our limbs freely.

In our new-found comfort I had a desperate desire for sleep, but the others would have none of it. It was still cold everywhere else in the ship and there was always the pos-sibility that the generator might fail. So Betelgeuse and Rigel drove themselves to the limit of endurance, trying all means of restarting the ION engine. Meanwhile Alcyone and I did what we could to cope with the rivers of water that came from the melting of ice and frost throughout every nook and cranny of the flight deck.

I became so engrossed in this task that it wasn't until I realized Alcyone had gone over to join the others at the main console that I knew another major step towards safety had been taken.

'Is it working?' I asked.

'Yes, at very low thrust,' answered Rigel.

'Not enough to pull the hawser away?'

'No. It would be dangerous to do so. We would lose the whole bulkhead,' Betelgeuse explained. 'It will be interesting to see what the Yela does now,' he added.

I could have made a pretty good guess at what the Yela would do, but again I desisted. In any case we were not left long in doubt. While Alcyone prepared a meal we were much in need of, we found ourselves gradually falling to the floor of the flight deck. Once again we were under acceleration.

'I keep wondering why the Yela has need of power from our ION engine. You'd think there would be self-contained generators of some kind,' I remarked.

'I'm sure there are,' answered Rigel, munching slowly on the leaves that Alcyone had somehow provided. 'But there has been damage. One part of the Yela's power-to-drive feed-back has been destroyed.'

'So an external source is needed for that part.'

'I think so.'

As we ate I became more and more sleepy, until I found it impossible to remain awake any longer. The others continued, however, to make tidying-up operations to the flight deck. Their life in space, and the lives of their ancestors, had fitted them much better than a terrestrial human to long periods of sleeplessness. By the time I awoke, more than fifty hours later, the flight deck was in good order. Alcyone and Betelgeuse were by now asleep, but Rigel still maintained watch at the console desk.

'I wondered how long it would be before you awakened,' he said.

'I can take over now. You must be just about dead on your feet.' My remark made me realize that the pressure had increased considerably. The Yela had evidently stepped up the acceleration. Where to, and why?

'There is not too much to do, not for the moment. Later

we will clean up the main body of the ship, once we are all rested.'

'How about the external sensors?'

'We will try to get those working also.'

Rigel was obviously very weary indeed, so I restrained myself from asking further questions. Quickly he curled himself up on one of the bunks. Within seconds he too was asleep – just like pressing a switch.

For the first time I would have liked to go off exploring through the ship. I had never enjoyed moving through the seemingly interminable maze of corridors, hatches, of laboratories and engine-room controls. Not that I would have enjoyed it now. But I was curious about the condition of the ship. I was curious to know if the ship could be made fully operative again. Since it was out of the question for the time being to leave my post at the control desk, I busied myself with working out the precise state of all the ship's systems, at any rate as far as could be deduced from the information now on display.

I found the life-support main system to be operative, not only on the flight deck, but through a fair body of the ship. It was not operative, however, in the region of the airlock or in the region of attachment of the hawser. This would mean taking to our space suits if we were to attempt once again to sever the hawser. We would need to use our intercom, permitting the Yela to read our thoughts. Interesting.

Then I began to wonder about the black sky I had seen in the brief moment outside the airlock. I puzzled hard about it and was led to make extensive calculations in which the acceleration of the Yela ship assumed important proportions.

I was still thinking hard about the calculations when Alcyone awoke. She came silently to my side. 'What are you working on, Dick?' she asked finally.

'Just an idea. Nothing, really.'

'It didn't look like nothing. You were scowling furiously.'

'Oh, well, something might come of it, I suppose. I wasn't getting anywhere, really.'

'Has anything happened?'

'Not so far as I'm aware. I would have liked to make a tour of the ship.'

'We'll do that soon. I think there will be very much to do.'

We waited for some hours for Betelgeuse to awake, talking to pass the time. It was easier now than it had ever been before to ask about the beliefs and the philosophy of life of the space people to whom she belonged.

'No, we don't have a religion in the sense you would understand it,' she began. 'To us, survival might be said to be a religion in itself. We have a strong code of behaviour, one to another, but since this applies mainly within flight, when our fleet is together, this is something that is hard to describe.'

'Because we are alone? This ship is alone.'

'Yes. Being a single ship in this way is strange, even to us. We might be alone for a limited time but not for the whole of a vast voyage, as we may be now.'

'Are you frightened?'

'Of being just a single ship?'

'Not so much that. Of what the end might be.'

'We do not know the end. How can I be frightened of what I do not know?'

'Well, frightened the ship might become explosively unstable?'

'If by being frightened you mean being impelled to do whatever is to be done, as an absolute priority, well then – yes, I am frightened.'

'But only if something is to be done?'

'Of course. Otherwise what would be the point of being frightened?'

'Would your will to survive force you to continue, even in the hands of the Yela?'

'That I find difficult to answer, but I think not.'

I thought of the hawser, connecting us to the Yela ship. We were headed for the territory of the Yela, where else? I wondered if I could ever persuade Alcyone to fight this thing through, to overcome what amounted to a deeply ingrained superstition of the Yela, a superstition that had obviously been imprinted on her from earliest childhood.

'We'll face that when it comes,' I concluded rather weakly.

'What is this which must be faced?' asked Betelgeuse. Awake now, he must have heard the last part of our conversation.

'Oh, nothing. We were just talking – more or less at random,' I answered, feeling embarrassed.

'There is much now to be faced,' went on Betelgeuse. 'I will take over the control, while the two of you make a patrol through the ship. There will be much work for all of us.'

'And Rigel?'

'We will let him sleep. He has been under a great strain this past thousand hours.'

'What are we to do?'

'I want a complete report on the state of the ship. Alcyone knows what has to be done.'

Our first job was to check that no chemical fuel was escaping from the main tank. Now that the ION engine was operative again, Rigel had cut out the standby system which had served us so well. Our store of chemical fuel was no longer being depleted – assuming there were no leaks, which was just what we had to test. Luckily, the route to the fuel tank lay through the part of the ship in which the life-support system was functional. Consequently this first bit of our task could be accomplished without the need to put on our recently discarded space suits.

I was amazed at how quickly the ice had disappeared from this part of the ship. With the exception of a few pools of water, which had accumulated in places where exit valves had become stuck, all the water had drained back into storage tanks. The metalwork was now quite dry and, being thoroughly rustproof, would be none the worse for our recent experience.

The rest of the ship was quite a different matter. The ice-coated caverns were still there. We explored as best we could, in our suits again. Now we had light to work by, we were no longer weightless, and our support packs were fully charged. Even so, I found this part of our job to be less than pleasant – recent memories of floating helplessly in those same icy caverns were still strong.

When we passed close by the airlock, Alcyone's voice came over the intercom. 'Dick, d'you think we should examine the possibility of cutting the hawser? We must do something about it sooner or later.'

'It think it is probably too late.'

'Too late for what?'

'The drive of the Yela ship is much stronger than our own engines. I think we may have accelerated to such a speed that we could never decelerate again.'

'You mean we need the Yela ship to supply sufficient deceleration?'

'That's right. The creature needs power from us and we need drive from it. I'm afraid we're mutually dependent.'

'I don't find that a pleasant thought,' said Alcyone wryly.

As we made our way back to the flight deck I kept wondering how far all this might not be true. I had thought it as well to make up a story to head Alcyone away from the idea of cutting the hawser, for I had no wish to have the Yela interfering with our life-support system again. It had not escaped me that we would probably have to use the intercom in any such operation and that the Yela would therefore be forewarned of it. Besides, my story could be true, especially if the time readings on our clocks were false. So much on this trip had turned out to be false. Perhaps the time we had spent in our curious hypnotized state had been much longer than we supposed. The idea had interesting possibilities, which occupied me until we rejoined Betelgeuse on the flight deck.

Betelgeuse had been working on the optical monitors, and he had just been joined by a sleepy-eyed Rigel.

'Dick, you're exactly in time,' he exclaimed with more enthusiasm than he'd shown for a long time. 'We should be getting some external data quite soon.'

'How's that?'

'All the components seem to be functional. We've only got to string them together now.'

At this, Rigel gave a monstrous yawn. I suspected Betelgeuse must have awakened him after all.

We all clustered around the monitor. Betelgeuse made various final adjustments.

'Check again that all components are operational.'

'All components operational,' answered Rigel after carefully examining a formidable complex of instruments.

The monitor remained dark.

'Strange,' grunted Betelgeuse, 'I'd swear everything is fully operational.'

'I told you, didn't I? It's black. The sky is as black as hell,' I exclaimed.

'I suppose you did,' acknowledged Betelgeuse, 'but I'm afraid I didn't believe you.'

'What direction are the sensors pointing towards?' I asked, ignoring the insult.

'Towards the rear – with respect to our motion.'

'Turn them forwards, dead in line with our motion.'

I waited while Rigel made the adjustments. As the sensors turned, he announced the angles to the line of motion in 10-degree steps.

170 degrees, 160 degrees . . . 30 degrees, 20 degrees.

The sky remained black.

10 degrees.

Still the sky remained black. Then suddenly a blaze of

light filled the screen, to be followed once again by black-ness.

'Bifusticator!' roared Betelgeuse.

'The screen burned out,' I shouted.

'No, the amplifiers have experienced a massive overload. But they are fully protected,' said Rigel in a puzzled quiet voice. 'It will take a moment or two for them to become operative again.'

'Turn the gain low!' instructed Betelgeuse.

'Of course,' agreed Rigel, sucking his teeth.

A wholly fantastic picture formed itself on the screen. Ahead of us, in the direction of motion of the ship, was a dense cluster of stars, each of them shining with an incredible steely-blue brilliance. I listened in chilled silence to the shouts and exclamations of the others. Something was dreadfully wrong here, not the stars, something else. The Yela ship should have been ahead of us. The great sphere of the Yela should be blotting out the centre of the star cluster. But no such silhouette was to be seen. The Yela was no longer ahead of us.

9   Flight Through the Galaxy

'Where is the Yela ship?' I asked.

The others crowded the screen. In astonishment Rigel exclaimed, 'We're free! I don't know how it happened but we're free again.'

Betelgeuse hummed and grunted. I remained doubtful and I said so, while Alcyone simply went on staring at the monitor.

'Well, there's one way to find out,' Rigel went on.

'How?'

'By checking the hawser at the bulkhead.'

'The life-support system isn't working in that part of the ship. It means using a suit and a pack.'

'I know,' Rigel nodded, 'I'll get on with it right away.'

I was quite happy for Rigel to take the job, since by now I'd developed quite a neurosis about being cooped up in the heavy awkward suits. More and more the damned things seemed to me like potential coffins, although I had to admit that they had saved my life more than once. Besides there were a few calculations I wished to make. I had a hunch things weren't by any means as simple as they seemed. Betelgeuse took over duty at the console, Alcyone continued her apparently never-ending job of putting to rights the hundred and one small things that still needed attention, while Rigel set off on his solitary mission to the airlock and to the bulkhead, where the hawser was attached. Idly almost, I continued doodling and scribbling. As often happens in such circumstances, the critical idea occurred to me in a flash – in so short a time that I could not have estimated it, a fraction of a second, no more. I calculated in earnest now, no more doodling.

I was still immersed in a sea of mathematics when I became aware of a commotion about me. Rigel had returned. He staggered on to the flight deck and just collapsed totally. Betelgeuse and Alcyone struggled frenziedly to get him out of the tightly fitting suit, which evidently was impeding his breathing. I joined the others, and the three of us eventually tore him free of the awkward accoutrements.

'What happened?' I asked.

'No idea,' snapped Betelgeuse.

'He has suffered a deep shock,' said Alcyone. Indeed there was a look of stark fear on Rigel's face. He was trying urgently to tell us something but could only manage to make a chattering sound with his teeth.

'Is he cold?' I asked again.

'Yes, cold with shock. Not cold with cold,' replied Alcyone. I knew what she meant. Betelgeuse handed her a syringe, with which she proceeded to give Rigel a shot of some drug, which judging from its immediate effect must have been pretty potent. We carried the unfortunate fellow to a bunk and placed him in a kind of electrically heated sleeping bag.

'I would have said that Rigel was just about the most phlegmatic person I've ever met. I wouldn't have thought anything in the world could have disturbed him like that,' I stated flatly.

Betelgeuse nodded gravely. 'That is what I would have said too.'

'He never batted an eyelid, even at the worst moments.'

'This was not a physical thing,' broke in Alcyone. 'It was something different.'

'Different?'

'Yes, different. Do not ask me what. But it was different. This isn't physical. It is in the mind.'

Betelgeuse kept nodding. 'Alcyone knows. She has seen these things before,' he said in his deepest bass tone.

'Perhaps the ship is broken, at the bulkhead.'

'Perhaps. We must find out. I shall go myself.'

'No, I'll go. You're the captain. You belong here.'

'Dick is right there,' agreed Alcyone.

Betelgeuse grunted. 'It is not good to ask Dick to do what I would not like to do myself,' he said.

'I've no doubt you would go yourself,' I smiled, 'but it doesn't happen to be the sensible thing to do. I shall go. After all, I've been through the airlock enough times by now.'

'That is true. But be careful. Remember to follow the procedure carefully.'

'Don't worry. I'll do that.'

The procedure for putting on the space suit, adjusting the support pack and going through decompression had by now become quite a reflex, very different from my clumsy beginning at the time of takeoff, so long ago. But although I had become more expert at it, I liked the routine even less than I had done at first.

I have explained several times that the main life-support system was operative only in a restricted part of the ship. The rest, which began at Q deck, was a wholly different world, a zero-temperature world without air, or so near to being without air that it made no difference. This part of the ship did not include any sensitive equipment, but it was much of the total volume of the ship. Storage space, which was large, and the space between the inner and outer skins of the ship all belonged to it. My task now was to explore this other part of the ship, not cursorily but in detail, to discover what it was that had so discomfited the unfortunate Rigel.

I had not been long on the job when Betelgeuse's voice crackled on the intercom. 'Dick, Alcyone has insisted on following you. She will meet you at the junction of U corridor with S deck, close to the alpha column. Over.'

'What's the idea? I can manage alone.'

'She thought it would be better if there were two of you, and I agree with her. Over.'

'O.K., then. I'm on my way. Over. Roger.'

This meant retracing my steps to a degree and I wasn't too pleased about it. The pressure was quite strong, and heaving the space suits about the awkward bends and ladders wasn't at all easy. Under normal operational conditions one wasn't intended to do this kind of thing. Normally, the life-support system functioned everywhere throughout the ship, so that work could proceed without encumbrance, not with the inefficiency of my present stumbling efforts. Clumping about in oversize boots wasn't the worst of it. I found the loss of dexterity in the hands particularly irritating. One had to fiddle around for minutes to do a simple job that normally would have taken only seconds. Anyway I'd be glad to have Alcyone along with me, I decided, as I negotiated the hatchway into Q deck. It would be less difficult for two of us to make a satisfactory tour of the ship than for me alone.

I found her waiting beside the alpha column. She came heavily toward me with a staggering motion.

'The oxygen cylinder. There's something wrong with it.' I heard her voice softly on the intercom.

'I'll switch to the spare cylinder,' I answered. Because it is impossible to make any deft adjustments while dressed in a heavy suit, the switch to the spare oxygen supply was a simple press-button affair. Quickly I sought to make the exchange but the button didn't move. This was always checked carefully as standard routine whenever we took out a support pack. I couldn't understand it and there was little time to think about what might have happened. I thumped the damned device, but still not the slightest movement, not a millimetre. The thing was frozen solid.

'I can't breathe. I can't . . . ,' came Alcyone's strangled voice, now in terror. I thumped still more fiercely on the support pack. I tried fiddling with the tubing from the oxygen supply but I was hopelessly inept. Alcyone's gasping was broken with short despairing cries. Convulsively she sought to tear away the visor from her helmet. I tried to stop her, for then the last hope would be gone. Suddenly I could see her face, convulsed in dying agony, with the lips blue and the face dark. Overpoweringly, I had the desire to open up my own helmet, with the crazy idea that my oxygen supply might suffice for both of us. As I fumbled with my support pack a voice within me, my own voice but strangely distorted, cried out for me to stop, to save myself. Exposed to zero pressure I would instantly become unconscious. Both of us would then be dead. Nothing would be gained by this, the voice cried out. I stood there while Alcyone died, ashamed to my innermost being. Coward ... coward ... coward ... I kept muttering to myself. I tried to drag her inert body, heavy in the suit, along the corridor. This too was obviously hopeless. After all the objective dangers we had gone through together, this was all so cruel and unnecessary. I cursed my stupidity. I cursed the fates, and lurched my way back towards the flight deck – alone.

After compression, I kept on my suit, since we would all have to return to the alpha column. Betelgeuse, Rigel and I would return there, to drag Alcyone's body to the flight deck. If we were quick enough there might be a chance of restarting the heart. I burst into the flight deck itself, feeling there wasn't a second to lose.

'Quick,' I shouted to Betelgeuse, 'Alcyone is out there. Her support pack has failed.'

'But Alcyone is here,' answered Betelgeuse calmly.

'She isn't. She's out there. Dead!' I shouted again.

'No, she is here. In the galley.' And indeed there she was, without any suit or support pack. As she came towards me, my teeth began to chatter uncontrollably. The room became grey and then suddenly black.

I awoke some hours later with my mind strangely diffuse. The space suit was gone. Lying on a bunk with my eyes closed, I tried to recapture the recent past. Vaguely I knew I must have been given a shot of some drug. The right thing to do would be to relax, to forget. But it was not in my temperament to leave corners of my own mind unexplored. I had to know what happened, and so I struggled, perhaps unwisely, to remember. As a lighthouse flashes out into the twilight, a memory of Alcyone's darkening features came on me.

'Alcyone!' I croaked, sitting upright on the bunk. 'Out there in the corridor, by the alpha column.'

'Alcyone is here,' I heard Betelgeuse say in a quiet, gentle voice. And indeed Alcyone again came from out of the galley. Without doubt it was she.

'But she's dead,' I protested, 'out there by the alpha column.'

Alcyone came to me, took me by the shoulders and gave me a slight shake, and said as she looked me in the eyes, 'Dick, do I look to be dead?'

'But out there you were just as real as you are now.'

'Rigel was out there. You remember.'

'It was because of Rigel that I went myself.'

'That's right. Rigel now calls it the Land of Hallucinations. Out there.'

'We have heard of it before, in our history. A reality that is not real,' explained Betelgeuse gravely.

'Where is Rigel now?'

'Asleep. You must sleep also,' said Alcyone firmly, picking up a syringe.

'No, no,' I said hoarsely, but in a strong voice. I heaved myself unsteadily from the bunk to prevent the injection.

'I prefer to face it out.'

'You are very stubborn.'

'A reality that is not real,' I murmured. Then I remembered the voice speaking from within myself, urging me to preserve my own life. Was that voice somehow aware of

108

the hallucination? Was there an inner core within myself that had remained undeceived? I turned to Betelgeuse. 'You mean that if we returned to the alpha column we should find nothing there?'

'I do not know what we should *imagine* we found there.'

'But why should there be reality here on the flight deck and not there by the alpha column?'

'It is the way of the Yela, to keep us from visiting that part of the ship.'

I remembered our earlier strange experiences, even before we met up with the Yela ship. Yet there had been nothing in those earlier events to compare with the astringent terror of my recent experience.

'But if the Yela can produce this sort of thing, why did it bother with the life-support system – interfering with it? Why was it so crude before?'

'Remember we are dealing with a disabled creature, Dick. Perhaps something in the creature is working now that wasn't working before.'

'I wouldn't like to be dealing with a fully healthy Yela then.'

'You are beginning at last to understand,' said Alcyone quietly and gravely, as she attempted to lead me back to the bunk.

'No, I'll be all right,' I replied somewhat brusquely. 'I'd like to take another look at the optical monitors.'

'You should rest. Your nervous system has received a severe shock.'

'It will be better for me to face it consciously,' I insisted.

'But perhaps not better for us,' grunted Betelgeuse. 'If you were one of my own people I would order it.'

'I want to see the optical monitors,' I persisted.

'Very well, but I don't think you will get much consolation from them.'

It was on the tip of my tongue to say that it wasn't consolation I wanted but understanding. I desisted, realizing that both Betelgeuse and Alcyone were frightened, frightened by what had happened to Rigel and to me, and perhaps frightened by the thought that we might go totally insane at any moment.

To humour me, Betelgeuse switched on the optical monitors, directed once again in the direction of the ship's motion. There again was the compact cluster of brilliant steely-blue stars. Once again there was no sign of the Yela ship.

'Is that real, or is it a hallucination?' I asked.

'What?'

'The absence of the Yela ship.'

'I don't understand it.' Betelgeuse shook his head vigorously. 'The Yela has gone. Yet the Yela is here. Otherwise how could there be hallucinations?'

'You think the Yela is here? In this ship?'

'How are we to know?' Betelgeuse shrugged his shoulders.

So this was why the two of them were so apprehensive. They thought the Yela might be lurking in our own ship, just as I had done myself in the early days of the voyage.

'I doubt it,' I said firmly. 'The Yela's influence is here all right, but not the creature itself.'

'How do you know that?'

'I don't know it. I suspect it. I'd like to turn the sensors around, to point in the opposite direction.'

'Opposite to our motion.'

'That's right.'

'But there's nothing to be seen there. The sky is dark. You said it yourself.'

'Even so I'd like to take another look.'

Sure enough the sky was quite dark. Nothing at all was to be seen.

'What does it mean?' whispered Alcyone.

'Let's find out. Switch on the searchlights.'

'Why?'

'Just a hunch.'

'I do not like hunches, I tell you, Dick.'

Betelgeuse was obviously nervous, as if he felt that by putting on the ship's lights he would somehow be declaring our position – as if this were not known already!

'Will you switch on, or shall I?'

With this challenge to his authority, Betelgeuse gave the necessary electronic commands, and as he did so the Yela ship appeared on our screen. The orange sphere lay there shimmering in our lights.

'It's very simple,' I said. 'We're not accelerating now. We're decelerating.'

Betelgeuse came instantly to life, shaking off his superstitions. 'That is easy to verify, by determining the orientation of the ship.'

It will be recalled that the optical sensors were telescopes, mounted not on the ship itself but on platforms that could be directed several kilometres away from the ship. The telescopes were then lined up with respect to our motion, which was not necessarily the same as the orientation of the ship itself. Under acceleration the ship pointed in the sense of motion, but under deceleration the ship was turned around, with the sense of motion pointing astern. It was this orientation that Betelgeuse now proposed to check. He was away from the monitor for a few seconds. He returned nodding vigorously.

'You're right, Dick. That star cluster lies astern, not in the direction of our bow. Everything has been turned around.'

'I understand the reason for the star cluster, and for why the other part of the sky is dark,' I announced triumphantly.

'Not a hallucination?'

'No, not a hallucination. It's just straightforward relativity. We're moving very fast, much faster than we thought, close to the speed of light.'

Betelgeuse pointed at the master clock. $T+5176$. 'There hasn't been sufficient time for us to attain such a speed.'

'The time isn't correct,' I persisted.

'There is no indication of the clock's having stopped.'

'Either it stopped, or one of us set it back.'

'Why would anyone do that?'

'Without knowing it, I mean.'

'Another hallucination?'

'Yes, another hallucination. Our flight has been much longer than that. At least three times longer.'

Betelgeuse was unconvinced. He went over to Alcyone who was again working in the galley. 'Dick thinks the clock is wrong,' he explained.

'How could that be?'

'I don't know.'

Then Alcyone took Betelgeuse by the arm and led him to where I was standing by the console and by the clock.

'You know,' she said, 'Rigel was examining the clock. Before he went out there.'

We all looked over to the bunk where Rigel was sunk in deepest slumber.

'I wonder what he was up to. Going out there. He must have done it for some purpose,' I said.

Betelgeuse, searching around, eventually found a bunch of papers. 'When he came back he had these papers in a pocket of his suit. Because of his condition I didn't trouble myself about them,' he explained.

I flipped over several sheets, and then came across four low-dispersion spectrograms, obviously of stars. Three showed no lines at all. The fourth had familiar absorption lines, the Balmer lines of hydrogen and H and K of calcium. But the standard comparison lines were peculiar. Their pattern was different from one spectrogram to another. This gave me the clue as to what Rigel had been up to. I pointed to one of the spectra. 'Look, the comparison lines here are in the normal position.'

'But there is nothing in the star, except continuum light,' exclaimed Alcyone in a puzzled voice.

'And there's still nothing here,' I said, picking up a

second sheet, 'even though the comparison lines are now in the ultraviolet.'

'I begin to see what you're getting at, Dick!' exclaimed Betelgeuse.

I pointed at the third negative case. 'I don't recognize comparison lines, but I think we'll find they are in the X-ray region.'

Betelgeuse picked up the fourth spectrogram, the one with the hydrogen and calcium lines. 'And the comparison lines are still further into the X-ray region here. I can see it,' he exclaimed. 'Rigel was taking spectra further and further into the short-wave region.'

'Until he found normal lines in the star's spectrum,' I added.

'Which implies a motion towards the star very close to light. Just as you said, Dick.'

'This is a star in the group ahead of us, in the direction of our motion?' asked Alcyone.

'I'm assuming it to be,' I replied. 'Otherwise there would be no explanation for the enormous blue shift of these hydrogen and calcium lines.'

Betelgeuse walked about the flight deck deep in thought. At length he turned to the two of us as we continued to study Rigel's spectra. 'This means of course that our journey is very much longer than we supposed it to be.'

'In the order of a hundred light-years,' I replied.

'How d'you arrive at that?' asked Alcyone.

'Oh well, from the blue shift of the Balmer lines. H α would normally be at a wavelength of more than 6,000 angstroms. Here, with this enormous blue shift, it's less than 60 angstroms. So we've got a relativistic dilatation of at least a hundred.'

'Which means, of course, that if we've been in flight for a year we must have travelled about a hundred light-years,' concluded Betelgeuse.

'At any rate we shall have by the end of deceleration,' I agreed.

'I can never quite believe in this relativity dilatation,' said Alcyone, shaking her head doubtfully.

'There's a very simple rule,' I told her. 'Just multiply the local time elapsed by the dilatation factor. This gives the distance travelled.'

'I know, but I still don't believe it.'

'We shall see.'

Betelgeuse held up a hand. 'This has most serious consequences,' he announced gravely. 'We can no longer decouple ourselves from the Yela. If we were to do so now we would have no means of decelerating to normal speed, since our ION engine is much less powerful than the Yela. And if we should wait until deceleration is completed and then succeed in decoupling ourselves . . .'

'We should be unable to return!' broke in Alcyone.

'Within our lifetimes,' I concluded.

'The situation is most serious,' grunted Betelgeuse. 'It is entirely outside my experience.'

I went over to the optical monitor and pressed the controls until the brilliant group of stars appeared ahead. 'Of course it is the same relativistic dilatation that is causing the rest of the sky to appear dark. We are getting enhancement in the forward direction.'

'In a cone?' asked Alcyone.

'Yes, a cone with a half-angle of only about a degree. The stars are bluer within the cone, and much more brilliant – except most of their light is now outside the visible range. They must be incredibly bright in the far ultraviolet.'

'It is remarkable that Rigel did not burn out his observing detectors,' agreed Betelgeuse.

'What we should do next,' I went on, 'is to identify these stars. What has happened is that stars from a wide angle over the sky have been compressed into an apparently dense cluster. The cluster will widen out again as we continue to decelerate.'

'These are our normal stars?' asked Alcyone.

'Yes, except that we are seeing them now in a remarkable way, because of our extreme speed of motion. What we must do is to relate them to our normal picture.'

'That is going to involve very accurate measurements,' nodded Betelgeuse.

'We can do it?'

'Oh yes, but we shall need much care.'

'Since we know the distances of many of these stars, we can determine our position.'

'By judging the angles?'

'Yes, the aberration angles will be somewhat different from one star to another. By doing a really careful job we can find out exactly where we are and what speed we are travelling at.'

I thought of beginning a program of measurement there and then, but by now the reaction from shock was setting in. 'Except that I'm going to have a good long sleep before I get down to work,' I concluded.

'That would be very wise,' agreed Alcyone. 'I will make arrangements for you to have a third-degree sleep.'

To my ear this didn't sound particularly attractive but I knew she meant better than she spoke. So I turned to one of the bunks. She brought me a large yellow pill, which I washed down with a glass of some kind of synthetic juice. Just like breakfast in a drug store. How far away the Earth had become in time and space, in motion and in my mind, I thought as I lay down to rest. Within minutes I fell into the deepest sleep.

By the time I awoke, some forty hours later, Betelgeuse and Alcyone were asleep, and Rigel was back on duty. He was busily engaged in calculating, with papers scattered around him.

'Discovered anything?' I asked.

'Identification program,' he answered tersely, by which I knew he was relating present measurements with the normal situation. In effect he was compiling a catalogue of the clustered stars and was comparing it with the usual catalogue.

'Are you able to use the computer?'

'Seems so.'

'No reason to suspect any difficulties?'

'Not so far.'

This was good, as it would reduce the labour of calculation enormously.

In spite of Rigel's concentration on the job I managed to insinuate myself into his program. Gradually, we arrived at an understanding of the external world as we were now seeing it. During the course of the many arithmetical calculations, I came on what at first seemed to be an error. I found a particular star to be too bright and by a margin that seemed too great to be attributed to an earlier error of measurement. Faced with the discrepancy we decided to make new observations and then to calculate *de novo*. The exercise cost us several hours of additional work and at the end of it we seemed only to have a further error as a reward for our labours. We were now finding the star to be even brighter than either of the two previous determinations. After arguing in a puzzled way for some time, Rigel said, 'Could it be the star that is changing?'

'A nova or a supernova?'

'Well, suppose all our determinations are really correct, what then?'

'Then we have to suppose the star is twice as bright as it was only an hour or so ago.'

'But an hour or two in our time would be a hundred or more hours at the star.'

'Because of the dilatation?'

'Yes, and that would be about right for a nova or a supernova. Probably a supernova.'

Rigel spent several minutes consulting a large catalogue and comparing it with the voluminous sheets on which he had performed his calculations. It was a curious feature of all the space people – Betelgeuse, Alcyone and Rigel were all the same – that they wrote and figured much larger than most terrestrial people. They liked large sheets and they always wrote in whopping big characters. This forced them to shuffle about a good deal from one sheet to another in any extended calculation. When eventually Rigel had finished his investigations, I asked, 'Well, what have you found now?'

'The star is the one known to Earth people as γ Ursa Major.'

'What about it?'

'It is not at all the late evolutionary kind of star which one expects to become a supernova.'

I went over to look at Rigel's compendious book of stellar spectra. Sure enough, there was nothing in the spectrum of γ Ursa Major to suggest the incidence of explosive properties.

'Another mystery, then. We must keep a close watch on this chap.'

Keep a close watch on it we did. As the hours passed the star brightened for a while and then faded away. It was unlike a supernova, for nothing at all remained in the end. There was no incipient white dwarf residue and no incipient pulsar.

The others eventually awoke and joined us. After expressing momentary interest in our discovery, Betelgeuse remarked, 'Well, this is the least of our worries.'

In this he was to turn out quite wrong, for here at last was a clue to all the happenings that had overtaken us since we left the Earth. It was a clue also to our future, but that would have been very much harder to read than the meaning of our voyage to this point.

The hours passed by with more comfort and less incident than at any other time in the voyage. Quite apart from the accurate measurements we were now making it was easy to detect the steady reduction in our speed of motion, for the dense bunching of the stars ahead of us began to lessen. The stars spread out over the sky, moving towards their normal positions. It was clear that our destination would soon be reached.

Even though we used ultraviolet and X-ray measurements, we were unable to detect any stellar residue from the star of U Ma. This had to mean that the whole star had somehow exploded and evaporated. We managed to verify that this was the case, the star having been replaced by an expanding nebula of gas. The surprise was to find the gas to be very cold, quite unlike the highly active shell of a supernova. In fact we had to use infrared techniques to detect it.

The mystery was compounded by two further absentee stars. As the normal pattern formed iself over the sky, we found a ninth-magnitude star in Cygnus to be missing, and also a medium-bright star in Cassiopeia. And we again found infrared expanding gas clouds where these two stars had formerly been. The situation baldly was that three stars had suddenly evaporated, for no apparent reason. We speculated a good deal on possible causes but none of us could come up with anything plausible.

We also had long discussions on our basic predicament, that even if we managed to unhook ourselves from the Yela we could not return, either to Betelgeuse's wandering fleet of ships or to the Earth. On the other hand if we continued to follow the Yela, we were certain to wind up exactly where none of us wanted to be, in the home of the Yela, for we had no serious doubt that it was to home base that the crippled Yela was heading.

The others favoured waiting until deceleration to low speed was essentially completed. Their argument was that we might still within our lifetimes be able to discover a planetary system moving around some star in the Ursa Major group. This seemed to me a long shot, but it would at least give us a motive, something to do, other than merely to survive. So I went along with the plan, although it called for what I now regarded as a thoroughly dangerous move. Betelgeuse had the idea of dealing with the Yela, not simply by disconnecting the hawser, which had caused us so much trouble, but of directing a broadside of torpedoes into the Yela ship. He argued that we could set the torpedo tubes manually and that such a procedure would remain unknown to the Yela. Then all we need do would be to throw a single switch. By the time the Yela discovered the situation it would be too late. The torpedoes would already be on their way. The plan sounded fine in theory, but after my experience with the Yela I had serious doubts about it. On the whole I would have preferred to let events take their course.

It was always a source of surprise to me that we never quarrelled together, even though we might disagree very strongly on issues of policy. I have no doubt this was because of the others, not because of me. Terrestrial humans, with lots of space at their disposal, had evolved into a thoroughly quarrelsome lot. But Betelgeuse and his people, accustomed to being together in the comparatively confined quarters of their spaceships, had developed a remarkably emotionless way of settling their differences. They reacted strongly to circumstances, in concert with each other, but not to arguments between them. They regarded tension between one individual and another as a thoroughly profitless way of dissipating their energies. Drama, in the terrestrial sense, did not exist for them.

It was agreed between us that Betelgeuse and I should do the heavy work connected with priming the torpedoes while Rigel concentrated on the electronics. This seemed fine at first, but by the time we came to the second bulkhead doorway my arms and back were aching badly. Betelgeuse was in his suit looking for a possible exit from the ship, one that we could use without going near the airlock or the hawser.

'How's it going?' he asked.

'Slowly.'

'Two more doors and you're in the armaments room.'

'Better keep your intercom switched off. Unless there is an emergency,' I suggested.

'It's lucky we can get at about a half of the torpedo tubes from our part of the ship,' grunted Betelgeuse. By 'our part of the ship' I knew he meant the unfrozen part, the part that the Yela hadn't sealed off.

'Why can't we open up the tubes from inside the ship?' Betelgeuse seemed to have developed what I took to be a quite irrational desire to find an exit that could replace the usual airlock.

'I don't like being sealed up inside my own ship,' he replied.

'Going outside under such strong deceleration will be very risky.'

'We shall wait until the deceleration is almost completed,' he replied.

Under strong acceleration or strong deceleration it would be possible to fall away from the ship just as catastrophically as a man might fall down a precipice. Not a comforting thought, being stranded in space with the ship rapidly moving out of range of our tiny jet packs. Normally we might expect to have the ship shut down its ION engine and then a pickup operation to be arranged without difficulty. No such rescue would be possible now, since it was the Yela engines that were in control. The more I thought about going outside the ship under these conditions the less I liked it.

Having adjusted his suit to his satisfaction, Betelgeuse went on his way, and I returned to the hard but straightforward task of forcing a route to the armaments room. A while later, Alcyone brought me some food, which I munched with some pleasure – essentially in relief from the hard work.

'You still don't like this torpedo idea?' she began.

'Not really. I would prefer to let events take their course.'

'Which would most certainly be bad.'

'We don't *know* that.'

'It is a fair inference.'

'I'm not so sure. What d'you make of those evaporating stars?'

'I think it must be something to do with the Yela.'

'Not a natural phenomenon?' I asked.

'No. I looked up the expected lifetimes of the stars that have gone missing. None of them was due for extinction by natural processes, not for many millions of years.'

'Very strange. I keep puzzling about it, whenever I take a rest from opening these damned hatches.'

'Poor Dick. Pretty soon you'd better get some sleep. There's no urgency about all this.'

'Maybe not. But when I start a job I like to get it done.'

'That is not a correct point of view. It is better to think only about the routine.'

'So you think the Yela has something to do with these stars? Why?'

'Why not? Whenever there is something bad, it is always the Yela.'

I laughed. How very similar to terrestrial behaviour, always to have a whipping boy at hand. 'I just can't see it,' I said. 'The amount of energy required to explode a star is fantastic. However technically advanced the Yela may be I just don't think it could produce enough energy.'

'Well, if the Yela isn't doing it, who is?'

'A good question. You know, it may sound a strange idea. But could the Yela be under some kind of attack?'

'How d'you mean?' asked Alcyone in some surprise.

'Not an attack by little creatures like ourselves, of course. But some much higher intelligence.'

'An intelligence that can remove stars?'

'That's the question I keep asking myself. I find it difficult to believe. But it does explain quite a bit.'

'Such as what?'

'Well, the sudden withdrawal from the Earth, for example. I know we took that to be due to our own actions. Setting up activity in the Sun and that sort of thing. But suppose the withdrawal was only a part of something much bigger. Suppose the whole of Ursa Major is under attack and that our friend out there is on his way home, hot-footing it to base camp.'

'Because the base is being attacked?'

'It's an idea, but don't take it too seriously,' I said.

'Blotting out stars sounds like Jupiter practising with Vulcan's thunderbolts. I think you'd better get some sleep,' concluded Alcyone with a kiss.

I went back to the flight deck and curled up on one of our improvised bunks. The next moment, it seemed, Rigel was shaking me by the shoulder.

'Can't a man get any sleep around here?' I grumbled, trying to curl myself into a still smaller ball.

'You've been sleeping for nearly ten hours,' was Rigel's caustic reply.

'What!' I exclaimed, sitting upright. 'What's left to do?'

'The torpedoes need loading into the tubes, the rear of the tubes need closing off, and the outer doors need opening.'

'How's your own work going?'

'I've set the torpedoes to manual control. They will have to be guided visually.'

'Mm,' I grunted unenthusiastically. 'Any interference from the sphere?'

'None, so far as I can see. Betelgeuse thinks it will be possible to go outside.'

'To open the outer doors of the torpedo tubes I suppose.'

'That's right. That's what he wants help with.'

I groaned again. This was just what I'd feared, the part of the job I didn't like.

'What's the deceleration now?'

'It's down to about half g.'

I braced myself hard with my legs against the flight deck and gave a few small springs. Half g, that's about what it felt like. From a muscular point of view this wasn't too bad, but it would be beyond the capacity of the jet packs to return us to the ship should we ever become separated.

'We shall have to remain attached to the ship,' I muttered.

'Betelgeuse is arranging to use magnetic grips.'

Magnetic grips, damn it. Space suits were awkward enough without having magnetic grips attached to them. I knew I wasn't going to like the next stage in the proceedings, not one little bit.

The torpedoes were laid out on a movable belt in front of each tube. Rigel had fitted a hand charge to fire the torpedo engines. The charge was triggered by a large lever attached to the side of the tube with a firing pin set in position exactly above where the charge would be on the torpedo. To reload, all that had to be done was to wind away on a secondary conveyor belt within the torpedo tube itself. This moved the next torpedo into its firing position. The arrangement was crude but simple.

It had been decided that Rigel and Alcyone were to put the final touches to this infernal system while Betelgeuse and I went outside the ship to operate the outer tube doors. I remembered how long ago in the early stages of the voyage I had been keen to volunteer for outside work and I wondered now in retrospect how I could have been so misguided.

By this time Betelgeuse had fitted up an exit route from our part of the ship that seemed to meet with his approval. It was nothing like as ambitious as the main airlock but it served our purpose. Once outside the ship we checked our time pieces and then made our way forwards using magnetic hand grips. It seemed unwise to make any use of our jet packs, since at all costs we had to avoid attracting the attention of the Yela sphere. Nor did we switch on the intercom system, which was much more of a nuisance – but we had it available in case of emergency.

On reaching the nose of the ship we took up positions over a torpedo tube door. Opening it proved difficult, more so than I'd anticipated. Whenever I pressed against the ratchet attached to the manual opening device, I simply rotated myself. Even locking my body against the ship didn't suffice, except to wrench my arm muscles. While I pondered what to do next, Betelgeuse appeared over the cylindrical curve of the ship. He shook his head and indicated that I should remain there while he returned to the exit point.

I waited a good while. Several kilometres away I could make out the Yela sphere, silhouetted dark against the star-dusted sky. Now that we were decelerated from our former rapid motion, the stars had spread out again over the sky, but their pattern was peculiar. Changing our position by rather more than a hundred light-years hadn't wholly altered the familiar constellations, but they were changed sufficiently to give me a curiously uncomfortable feeling. The biggest change was in the direction of Ursa Major itself, the direction of our journey. The whole of the Big Dipper had gone. In the opposite direction, on the other hand, constellations like Aquarius, Pisces Austrinus and Grus were still quite recognizable. It was this partial familiarity that was so disturbing.

I felt a sharp tug on my lifeline and practically jumped out of my skin – more precisely, I nearly came adrift from the ship. Betelgeuse was coming towards me carrying a bundle of power tools. He gave one of them to me together with its accompanying generator and pointed determinedly at the ratchet. I pushed the end of the tool hard against the ratchet and hopefully pressed a button, only to find myself spinning around like a catherine wheel. Although I couldn't see his face I knew Betelgeuse was laughing fit to bust. Eventually he stopped my rotary motion and placed my hand grip a little way from the ratchet point to which he tied my lifeline. Then he indicated that I should grip him around the waist. I started the tool again. We both moved but only slowly now. By changing his handgrip Betelgeuse managed to check the motion, and the ratchet at last began to turn.

When the first tube was opened we passed quickly on to the second. Hanging on to Betelgeuse's middle, although awkward, was much better than hand winding would have been.

On the fifth tube the tool ran out of puff, but Betelgeuse had brought a spare – this was the reason for the size of his load. Then, as he was changing from one to another, there came a scream of electronic chatter in my earpiece. For a moment I thought I must inadvertently have switched on the intercom, but Betelgeuse was getting the same frenzied message. Hastily, he indicated that we should finish opening the tube and then return to the interior of the ship.

It was while we were on the way back that the thing happened. The ship gave a violent lurch, completely breaking our magnetic holds. A gap opened up between us and the ship, which widened quickly with every passing second. My instinct was to start up the jet pack, but this would inevitably separate us.

'Betelgeuse!' I gasped. 'Where are you?'

I waited a long moment for his reply.

'Dick, we must find each other before we try returning to the ship. Start counting.'

So I began speaking as evenly as I could. 'One – two – three – four – five – six – seven – eight – nine – ten. One – two –'

Betelgeuse was more skilled in the use of the jet packs than I was. He would first locate my direction and then slowly close the distance between, as slowly as possible.

At length I saw the flame from his pack. I gave a quick flick on my own motor, so that he too could pick up my position visually. After another wait, seemingly for an age, he eventually floated gently by.

'What happened?' I asked.

'The torpedoes fired.'

'What!'

'It was the recoil from the torpedoes that kicked us off the ship.'

'But why?'

'I don't know. I cannot imagine Rigel having made a mistake.'

'Have we enough drive in these packs to get back?'

'Yes, so far as the torpedo recoil is concerned. I'm more worried by the drive from the Yela sphere. Besides we don't know where the ship is.'

This was just the problem which had been worrying me. Picking up the dark silhouette of the ship was going to be awkward, especially as its distance from us became greater. Normally during a space walk the ship's lights would be on, and normally the ship would not be on tow as it was now.

No sooner had these thoughts occurred to me than the first difficulty was resolved. The ship's lights came on. As far as I could judge, the ship and the Yela sphere were now twenty to thirty kilometres away. The gap must be widening every second. Unless something drastic could be done, we were certainly lost.

'You can see the torpedo trails,' said Betelgeuse in a surprisingly calm voice. Indeed, the lights had revealed three trails across the sky, disturbingly reminiscent of terrestrial condensation trails, except these were coloured red.

'I doubt if they hit anything,' I replied.

'That's just the point.'

'What?'

'I think they must have been fired by the Yela. You were right, Dick, we should never have engaged in anything so foolish.'

'No good worrying about it now.'

Suddenly Rigel's voice crackled in my earpiece. 'Betelgeuse, locate your position. Betelgeuse, locate your position . . .'

'Rigel, this is Betelgeuse. This is Betelgeuse. Over.'

'Betelgeuse, where are you? Over.'

'Dick and I are together. We were unhurt. A line from my eye to the ship is quite close to the globular cluster in the constellation of Hercules. You are about thirty kilometres away but your distance is increasing fast. Repeat. Your distance is increasing fast. Over.'

'We are preparing to attempt to cut the hawser. Hold your jet packs in reserve. Over.'

'Jet packs are being held in reserve. Suggest cut hawser from *inside* of ship. Otherwise more torpedoes may be fired.'

Alcyone's voice came excitedly in reply. 'Unidentified objects appearing behind Yela ship!'

'Turn the lights towards them,' I suggested.

We waited for a while, rotating slowly – except that it was the heavens themselves which seemed to be revolving about us. Then I saw it, and in the same instant I heard Betelgeuse exclaim, 'Gallfinder! It is another Yela ship.'

I watched as a second glimmering sphere appeared behind the first one. This second sphere was far more uniformly illuminated, for instead of its being smooth there were glinting objects and rings protruding from its surface. It looked something like Saturn.

'What the devil are all those?'

By way of a reply I heard Betelgeuse give one of his usual grunts.

We studied the apparition at some length.

'I think those are the Yela's external sensors,' Betelgeuse pronounced.

'For observation?'

'For observation of the world in all wavelengths – X-rays, ultraviolet, visual, infrared and radio. The Yela has complete electromagnetic vision.'

'So the Yela ship that brought us all this distance is now home again, among its own kind,' I said.

'It would seem so. We are now in Ursa Major, the territory of the Yela.'

I forbore to reply that we were also without a ship, with only a few hours of life-maintaining materials remaining in our packs. I could see little better prospect than being picked up by the new Yela ship, much as my companions dreaded such a possibility. All along I had had the suspicion it would come to this in the end. It seemed inevitable from the moment I had fastened the hawser, the hawser which was the cause of all our troubles. Without the damned hawser we might now be journeying comfortably with Betelgeuse's fleet of ships – or perhaps sipping a scotch and soda back home on Earth.

The sky was traversed by a racing flame. It came along one of the torpedo tracks. The track was now a brilliant violet colour, not the dull red glow of an hour ago. At first I thought it came from the new Yela ship. It came along the torpedo track and lit up our ship in a glorious corona of scintillating colours. Then a fiery streak of purple hurtled across from our ship to the first Yela sphere, as if Rigel and Alcyone had set off some new and deadly weapon. The Yela sphere flared out also in a corona, which maintained itself for a long moment, until at last gigantic coloured streamers burst in all directions.

We floated now in a world of brilliant light, searingly

brilliant light, covering a patch of sky where the Yela ship had been. The patch spread out rapidly until it covered all of the sky in the direction of our own ship. Then it spread until it was everywhere. As we continued to float and to turn, there was luminescence everywhere. I became aware that I was immersed in a vast river of moving gas, and at last I understood that the Yela had disintegrated. It was from the Yela that this great holocaust came, the Yela which had dragged us a hundred light-years from our course.

There was nothing to be done except to wait. We would float slowly apart but there would be little difficulty, once all this debris became dissipated, in finding each other again. If our ship was intact, we might even be able to return there, since the Yela was now gone and perhaps even the hawser too. The dancing light had somehow found the Yela, by working its way along the hawser. Just as the hawser had represented disaster for us, so in the end it had for the Yela. Where had the all-consuming light come from? From the second Yela sphere? Was one Yela now destroying another? There were plenty of questions to occupy me, besides the all-important one of what had happened to our own ship. I tried to raise Rigel and Alcyone on the intercom. Failure meant nothing in itself, for I couldn't even raise Betelgeuse, since the static noise was quite overwhelming.

At last I could see the background of stars again. I was surprised at the sense of relief that this gave. My plight was serious in the extreme, yet the return of the stars seemed to spell a kind of confidence in the future. It was remarkable how dependent I had become during the voyage on the star-studded background. Just as all our everyday physical processes are dependent on the background of the distant universe, so I had now become psychologically dependent on this same background.

As the static noise became less I tried repeatedly to establish communication with the others. At last I picked up a signal. Not a voice, but the space distress signal. The signal was very weak, which would make it difficult to locate accurately. I knew my lack of skill with the controls of the jet pack would almost surely lead to disaster should I attempt to home in on the signal manually, so there was nothing to do but to put my trust in the automatic control. In theory this was supposed to line up on a distress beacon and then to fire the jet-pack motor in such a way that one moved towards the beacon. The idea was to get one back to the ship, the distress signal from one's own pack serving to fire a beacon in the ship. So normally one would expect to be homing in on the ship, but now I had no idea of whether the signal was coming from the ship or from Betelgeuse. If it was from the ship the situation was bad, because its weakness would imply that the ship was very far away, in which case my jet pack would run out of fuel long before I could have any hope of reaching home. I would be left in space without having any means of controlling my motion.

I switched on the automatic homing system. In such a system one knows in what direction one is being pushed. Provided the push is always in the same direction it can be inferred that motion will also be in that direction. But if one receives pushes in different directions it becomes difficult to know the motion – this can only be done through a rough mental averaging of the different impulses. Motion itself produces no sensation.

This was my situation now. The automatic system started by hunting around, presumably because the distress signal was weak. I feared the whole of my fuel would become used up in an aimless random walk. But eventually the pushes in my back became predominantly in the direction of the distorted constellation of Sagittarius, so evidently the system had behaved rather like a homing pigeon. It had circled around until it was decided on the appropriate direction and then it had set out systematically in that direction.

But had it made the correct choice? I listened anxiously for the signals to become louder, which they eventually did – after what seemed an excruciating length of time. I decided that even a small subjective increase of signal meant that I had covered a fair fraction of the distance to their point of origin, whether Betelgeuse or the ship. I thought of trying the intercom again but decided against it, on the grounds that any messages would interfere with the automatic control of my jet pack.

The pushes in my back were now in the opposite direction to Sagittarius, which meant that I was being decelerated. The signals in my earpiece had become quite loud and I was tempted to switch to manual control. However tempting this might seem – on manual I could certainly have used the intercom – I decided finally not to try it. I had come so far trusting the automatic. I might as well trust it for the rest of the way.

This remained a reasonable judgement until the system began to hunt once more. The signal was loud and clear now, so I decided there would be no harm in making a shot at the manual control. I waited until the blee-bleep seemed to be growing stronger. Then I cut both the automatic and the motor. Switching on the intercom transmitter, I tried to raise Betelgeuse. After a few moments I was delighted to hear his voice.

'Bifusticator! But I'm glad to hear you, Dick.'

'What is the trouble? Over.'

'I've lost two of my fuel cylinders. Over.'

'Have you any motive power?'

'A little only.'

'Could you reach me? I don't think I'm very far away.'

'Give me a signal and I'll try.'

Within minutes Betelgeuse had manoeuvred himself close alongside. We tied ourselves together on a length of nylon line, which was something we should have done long ago.

'We must have been carried apart by the wind from that

131

great explosion,' grunted Betelgeuse. 'What did you make of it, Dick?'

'For some reason the Yela exploded.'

'And the ship?'

'I'm not very optimistic. There isn't any reply at all from the ship.'

'The fire would have destroyed all the external antennae.'

'The fire which destroyed the Yela?'

'Yes. The ship will now be blind.'

'Do you see how we can find it then?' I asked.

'No. I have given much thought in the last hour to that question. There is no way for us to find the ship, unless Rigel can make the transmitters work again. We must wait in hope of that.'

'How about the second Yela ship?'

'What about it?'

'Well, it escaped from the fire, I think. D'you think we could locate it?'

'What for?'

'Well, frankly, I don't want to go on floating around out here.'

'Perhaps that would be better than locating the Yela.'

'Except that the Yela may well have captured our own ship.'

There was a long silence while Betelgeuse thought about that one. Myself, I had no such scruples. To me, the Yela was nothing yet but a shimmering orange sphere – and a name. On the other hand, I knew I would never go off on my own. I would go only if Betelgeuse would go, and persuasion was likely to prove difficult.

'In any case we have no more idea where the Yela is located than we have of our own ship,' he said.

'We could both transmit a distress signal.'

'Why both?'

'To show that we have come together.'

'Why should the Yela be interested in that?'

'It would show that we are no longer seeking each other.'

There was a pause, broken eventually by another grunt from Betelgeuse.

'What is it?' I asked.

'Well, Dick, for a long time, while I was waiting for you to reach me, I examined the sky.'

'For what?'

'Suppose you answer that question yourself by looking towards Aquarius.'

I manoeuvred myself to the best arrangement for observing this part of the heavens. I couldn't stop myself from spinning, of course, but I was able to get the axis of my rotation oriented so that if one thought of it as a polar axis then Aquarius lay on the equator. In this situation I watched the heavens rotating round and around. At each revolution, as Aquarius came into view, I scanned a portion of it. Instead of looking over the whole of a fair patch of sky, mentally I divided the area into a grid, and at each revolution I examined one of the small units of the grid. After several hundred turns I found what I took to be the thing which Betelgeuse had spotted – an exactly spherical dark patch, somewhere around five arc minutes in diameter. I knew this to be the Yela occulting the distant stars. From the size of the dark circular patch I quickly estimated that the Yela must be rather more than five hundred kilometres away from us.

It was incredible that Betelgeuse had been able to spot the thing. I had found it hard enough, even though I had been told what part of the sky to examine. He had done it without any such information.

'I have it,' I said, 'not too far from δ Aquarius.'

'Right. We could start heading in that direction if you like. But not with the distress signal operating. I would prefer to remain hidden.'

Because we were so small, it would, of course, be very much harder for the Yela to spot us using a similar occultation technique. But with a radar technique I had no doubt the Yela would be able to detect us. Betelgeuse could not have been in much doubt about it either. He was simply bolstering up his courage to face what was entirely repugnant to him. Yet approach the Yela we must, since this gave the best chance of finding our own ship.

Drawing ourselves together on the lifeline, we managed to exchange jet packs. I preferred to leave the next part of the operation to Betelgeuse. He had had a lifelong training in space-walk techniques, beside which I was only a rank amateur. Before we set off towards the Yela sphere, I took good care to ensure that my lifeline was quite secure.

Eventually Betelgeuse was ready. I felt the pull in the lifeline, noting that it was in the general direction of Aquarius. We had spaced ourselves about a hundred yards apart, so that the exhaust gases on Betelgeuse's pack – my pack really – had reasonably dissipated themselves before reaching me. The pull on the lifeline was remarkably steady, implying far better control than I could have achieved. Provided the jet motor continued to function, we should manage to reach the Yela sphere in between one and two hours. I estimated that our life-support systems would continue for about twice as long as that. So we should reach the sphere just about in time – provided, of course, the Yela didn't decide to accelerate away from us.

I found myself wondering if we could have used the same technique for locating our own ship as we had done for the Yela, by searching the sky for a dark area having the shape of the ship. This would be more difficult because our ship was cylindrical. A dark circular patch had been easier to pick out. I reflected that Betelgeuse had almost certainly been searching for our ship but had found the Yela instead.

Then I began to consider the Yela itself. What was inside the shimmering metallic sphere. Was it all metal, a gigantic computer? These were questions I had thought about a hundred times before. The difference now was that pretty soon I was likely to have an answer to them.

The tug on the lifeline had been increasing for some time now. I was surprised that Betelgeuse was managing to get so much drive out of the small jet pack, and I was surprised that he wasn't being more sparing in his use of fuel. Perhaps he was afraid that the Yela might move away before we reached it? The tug increased even more, so much so that I rechecked that the line was still securely fastened. At length I decided to break our self-imposed silence on the intercom. 'What's the flaming hurry?' I asked.

'The drive is not due to me at all,' was Betelgeuse's astonishing reply. 'I have just switched off the motor. Yet the drive is still continuing.'

I could see the red glow on Betelgeuse's pack had disappeared. So he had certainly killed the jet motor.

'What the devil is it then?'

'I don't know. We seem to be falling towards the Yela. In some kind of field,' replied Betelgeuse.

'It could be a magnetic field,' I muttered, 'although it would need to be incredibly powerful.'

We could see the dark circular patch cast by the Yela sphere against the sky. It was now much larger – roughly four times the diameter than when we had first seen it – which meant that we had covered about three-quarters of the distance towards it. This still meant the creature was more than a hundred kilometres away. It was hard to see how it could produce a magnetic field at such a distance that would be strong enough to control our motion. But controlled we certainly were: the push was still increasing. I reckoned we might expect to reach the damned thing within about twenty minutes.

The circular dark patch of the Yela sphere became steadily larger and larger until eventually it blotted out the whole constellation of Aquarius the Water Gatherer. I wondered if we would simply crash at high speed into the sphere itself. Or would we whip around it in some kind of orbit? Nothing I could conceive of suggested a pleasant end to our journey.

In place of the large patch ahead there was suddenly a huge shining sphere – suspended, it seemed, in space. Lights had been switched on, illuminating the vast array of detecting devices we had already seen on our ship's sensors. These were now plainly visible to our unaided eyes.

'Looks as though we were expected,' grunted Betelgeuse.

'Quite a reception committee, isn't it?' I replied.

11   The Trapped Ship

The glittering sphere ahead of us quickly became still larger, until it filled about a quarter of the sky. We were now moving in an orbit wholly controlled by the field of the sphere, which I still took to be magnetic. The light was so bright that we lost our dark adaptation and consequently could no longer distinguish the background of the stars. It became necessary to judge our position from the rings that circled the sphere, and from the multitude of detecting devices that accompanied the Yela on its journeys. These, it seemed, were locked in position magnetically, at various neutral points in the field. Indeed I suspected that the field existed precisely to lock the various sensory devices in appropriate positions around the sphere.

We were now but a mile or two from the vast sphere itself. Time and again we swept around it, moving along a complicated path, which I could not begin to understand or to anticipate. We never seemed to make the same circuit twice. I could see that the rings didn't quite touch the sphere. In fact the surface of the sphere seemed entirely unbroken. It consisted of completely smooth metal, golden in its sheen. At first sight one might have supposed the interior of the sphere would be completely insulated from the exterior. But this could not be so. There had to be a highly complex system of currents flowing on the surface of the metallic sphere. These would be induced by the rings, in accordance with the information that was being acquired by the more distant sensory devices. The electric currents in the metal surface would then be subject to analysis by whatever lay inside the sphere – by the Yela itself, in other words.

'Gallfinder!' exploded Betelgeuse. 'Where are we going?'

'I think we're moving rather like a ball in a child's magnetic toy.'

'How would that be?'

'We shall go on round and round until we reach some equilibrium point.'

'Or we may go round and round forever. Which would be ridiculous.'

'I doubt it,' I replied. 'I've been watching carefully. We never go round twice along the same path. Sooner or later we'll get ourselves trapped by a couple of magnetic pinches.'

'Oroblatz! What d'you propose to do then?'

'I don't know. Wait until the support system runs out, I suppose.'

'Not a good prospect, my friend.'

'No. But you've always said that anything would be preferable to falling into the hands of the Yela.'

'I suppose so. But I would prefer to die in a more dignified way.'

Our path took us very near to what I took to be an enormous radio telescope. It had several thousand individual circular dishes apparently connected together, each about a hundred metres in diameter. Before I could consider the details further, we had swept past and were approaching a set of translucent cubical boxes. To my horror we headed for the interior of this curious arrangement, suggesting to my mind the possibility of a head-on collision with one of the boxes. I could see no reason for this strange device until we had in fact passed safely through it. Our speed had clearly been very markedly reduced.

'That was some kind of field control station,' I remarked.

'I think those boxes contained superconducting material,' agreed Betelgeuse.

At our reduced speed we took much longer to go around the orange-coloured sphere, which made it less difficult to examine details. I was concentrating on the surface of the sphere, which continued to fascinate me, when Betelgeuse exclaimed,

'The ship! Over there.'

On the Earth whenever anyone uses the phrase 'over there' to indicate an object of interest, he usually makes a manual indication of the direction with the hand. In space such an instinctive procedure is not possible. Consequently I had no idea of what direction Betelgeuse meant. Nor could he define it in relation to distant stars, since the background light, which evidently emanated from the surface of the sphere itself, prevented the stars from being seen. In any case Betelgeuse soon lost whatever it was he had observed.

'Are you sure it was the ship?' I asked.

'I am not usually mistaken in such things,' Betelgeuse replied in a grimly serious voice.

So we both continued to keep a sharp eye open for the ship, ignoring all else. I spotted it a while later, but only in a fleeting glimpse. The fact that we were spinning and following a complicated curved path, and that from time to time the rope between us would tighten, leading to an essentially discontinuous change in our individual motions, made any kind of sustained observations essentially impossible. But at any rate I'd seen the ship. Like Betelgeuse I hadn't any doubt about it.

'How are we going to get near enough to it? There's the problem,' I muttered.

'There indeed is a problem, my friend,' growled Betelgeuse.

Unlike simple linear motion, our present orbital convolutions could cause us to come quite close to the ship only to find ourselves barred from it by the walls of a magnetic bottle.

'The best plan would be to check our motion,' I suggested hopefully.

'How would that be?'

'If we could slow down, the eddy currents in our suits would be reduced,' I answered. 'It's these currents on which the magnetic field gets its grip.'

'You mean it would then need less of a force to enable us to cross the magnetic field?'

'That's the idea. The eddy currents must be entirely in the metalwork that we're carrying along with us – mostly in the jet motors, I would think. A little also in the life-support system.'

'We can't get rid of that,' grunted Betelgeuse.

'No, but we could dump my jet pack.'

'We can try that.'

It took a few moments' wrestling with the press button attachments of the jet pack for me to free myself. Instantly I felt much less under strain, but what I had overlooked was the imbalance that would immediately set up between the forces acting on Betelgeuse and on myself. This almost instantly led to a furious tightening of the line between us.

'Retrieve your pack!' I heard Betelgeuse shout in a strangled voice. With a desperate grab I just managed to catch hold of a webbing attachment. I could feel the line slacken as my arms tightened again on the jet pack.

'Oroblatz, but I was nearly suffocated then,' Betelgeuse gasped.

'We must check our motion before we try that trick again.'

'Check our motion?'

'Yes, with your jet motor. If we can reduce speed sufficiently, it may be possible to avoid generating a big tension in the line,' I explained.

'It will use up much of the remaining fuel.'

'I know. But what else is there to be done?'

'Gallfinder! We are dead mutton in any case. So I will try.'

The glow of the jet motor appeared once again on Betelgeuse's pack. For the most part he kept the rate of burn very low, except when our direction of motion was particularly well defined, as it was when for a while we moved directly towards – or directly away from – one of the Yela's sensory devices. At such times Betelgeuse would markedly increase the braking action of the jet.

We knew that we were slowing down, because it took longer and longer to make a significant change in our position. At length we decided it would be safe to try jettisoning all inessential metallic objects. At last I got rid of my jet pack and Betelgeuse contrived to rid himself of empty fuel cylinders. We even shed the empty cylinders from our support systems. It was depressing how little in the way of supplies of all kinds we now had left.

When we again located the ship it was lying farther away from the Yela sphere than we were. So we elected to burn part of the precious remaining fuel to increase our angular momentum about the sphere. We decided to increase the mean radius of our orbit until it was almost the same as that of the ship. This was about as much as we could expect to achieve. We would then have to rely on magnetic irregularities to produce precession of both our own orbit and that of the ship, hoping eventually for a close encounter to occur. We would then need the very last of our fuel to close the remaining gap between us and the ship.

The uncertain component of this plan was the length of time it would take for a suitable encounter to take place. We could only let events take their course, moving as little as possible to conserve oxygen. I forced myself to relax and I tried to make my mind go blank, for as soon as I started to think, my muscles would tense up, consuming more oxygen than was necessary. After longer than I had dared hope the support system would last, Betelgeuse's voice rasped harshly in my earpiece. 'I don't think we can expect the ship to come closer than it is at present. I'm going to make the attempt, my friend.'

Knowing there wasn't likely to be another opportunity, I waited and wondered how Betelgeuse could hope to navigate through a sea of magnetic forces whose form he did not know. Thinking we really needed a sophisticated computer capable of making suitable feedback calculations, I watched the bursts of red flame appear at the far end of the line. After each burst we seemed to rear ourselves over the crest of an invisible wave, sliding down a smooth surface into a new pocket of magnetic force.

The ship was certainly not far away now. The whole length of it was plainly visible, and the view was not encouraging, for the surface was evidently entirely smooth. There was no sign of any entrance or exit. I had the feeling that the outer skin must have been momentarily fused by the corona of fire that had imbedded it.

The trouble was that our progress over the waves was taking us much more parallel to the ship than towards it. Betelgeuse at length became totally exasperated. 'Bifusticator!' he roared. 'I will drive it through.'

There came an explosive outburst from the jet pack. The pull on the line increased as we seemed to climb a steep high wall. We lay there for a long moment and then began a slow stately fall towards the ship.

With a quickening of pulse and an unwise quickening in my breathing, I realized we were floating down to the same magnetic equilibrium point as that which was holding the ship. The ship was tightly held there because of its great metallic content. Had we not thrown away so much metal we would never have managed to penetrate the magnetic walls that held the ship so fixedly.

'Watch for impact,' yelled Betelgeuse.

We landed on the hull of the ship with the force of a parachute drop. Our motion perpendicular to the ship's surface was immediately checked in our legs and in the thump we received as we sprawled on the smooth metal. But we had no means of checking our motion parallel to the surface. We went sliding freely, still tied together by the lifeline, proceeding to orbit around the cylindrical body of the ship, with the magnetic forces preventing us from falling off again. In fact we were rather like a couple of tied satellites in orbit around our own ship. The metal was smoother than the smoothest ice. We simply went round and around and around, which struck me as just about the most ridiculous way to end one's career.

But of course there was a very slight degree of friction between our suits and the metal surface of the ship. In the long run this just had to slow us down. By the time we became aware that our motion was at last being checked – secularly, as astronomers would say – we must have done a good twenty complete circuits of the cylindrical surface.

We came at last to rest.

'Oroblatz,' spat out Betelgeuse, 'but that was a frenzy of a ride.'

I sorted myself out as best I could and said lugubriously, 'How are we supposed to get inside here? It seems the whole surface has been suddenly fused. Not enough to boil away the whole of the metal, but metal has flowed everywhere over the exits, over the airlock and over the torpedo tubes.'

Betelgeuse pointed far astern. 'Do you see what I see?' he asked.

I gazed in that direction and saw to my astonishment a line of winking lights stretching away into the distance. 'What the devil is that?'

'Just what I have been asking myself, Dick. You know what I think it is? I think it's a very long piece of wire. Bits of it are picking up the light.'

I stared for perhaps a couple of minutes and came to the opinion that this rather far-fetched idea could possibly be right. 'Where would the wire be coming from?'

'Here. The ship.'

'But why?'

'To pick up radio signals. Without something like that the ship would be blind.'

I took in the implications of this remark slowly. 'You mean Alcyone and Rigel might still be alive?'

'I do not see why not. It's true that an enormous electric current must have passed through the ship, but if it alternated rapidly enough it would have contained itself to only an outer skin of the ship.'

'With the interior shielded?'

'Yes, my friend, with the interior shielded.' There was a sense of triumph in Betelgeuse's tone and manner which I was not yet able to share.

'Shouldn't we be doing something about it?' I asked helplessly.

'We *are* doing something about it,' shouted Betelgeuse pointing at his helmet.

It took me a moment to realize what he meant. By using the intercom transmitters in our conversation we were generating radio signals, which Rigel should be able to pick up on his improvised antenna.

'Rigel! Rigel! Are you hearing us? Over,' thundered Betelgeuse.

We waited tensely for a reply. No voice came, but there was a sudden increase in the hiss of the noise in my earpiece. Then the noise broke itself into a series of pulses, which were evidently not generated naturally. For some reason Rigel must be lacking a suitable microphone.

'He's playing with the transmitter to gain control,' I said.

Betelgeuse held up his arm for me to maintain silence. 'Rigel, this is Betelgeuse. Dick and I are here together. We shall make our way to the point where you have managed to set up your wire antenna. We are going to find the place where the wire comes outside the ship. I am assuming this will be at the stern end. Is this correct? Over.'

From the pulses of noise which followed, Betelgeuse deduced that his assumption was correct. Together we began to make our way very gingerly along the ultrasmooth surface. After a long search we found the exit point of the wire antenna that Betelgeuse had so acutely spotted. Already Rigel was working to open up an entrance into the ship. He was using a cutting torch and taking a long time over it, I thought in some desperation, for my oxygen supply was near to its end. There was no doubt about it now. Remembering that I had switched cylinders in good time when the first one was nearing exhaustion, I went back to it now. I sat there on the smooth metal, breathing as little as I could manage. When Betelgeuse suggested that we might be of some assistance to Rigel, I could only point weakly to my helmet and remain sitting there.

A small hole in the outer skin of the ship appeared with agonizing slowness. By now I was getting very little oxygen, and a dull heavy thump was building up in my ears. I thought I heard Betelgeuse on the intercom, but the voice seemed dragged and distorted. There was no chance at all, I realized, of getting in through the hole – in our bulky suits that would involve a struggle in itself – and of then making my way through the body of the ship to the flight deck. My last thought was that one of us at least would make it to safety, which was something of an achievement.

The voice came back again, calling me from the end of a long tunnel. The tunnel was narrow and it constricted my chest painfully as I tried to crawl along it. I couldn't distinguish what it was the voice was saying, but I knew it to be urging me to escape from the tunnel. The pain in my chest worsened. I longed above all else to be able to stop crawling, to rest for a little while. But the hollow voice was louder now and it wouldn't permit me to rest.

Firecrackers burst in my eyes. An active centre in my brain told me that I wasn't dead yet. I was sufficiently curious to wonder why. Why wasn't I dead? I should have been. I saw a vague shape standing over me and knew it to be Betelgeuse.

'I'm all right,' I gasped.

'He's come round,' said Betelgeuse to Rigel. Then he pushed me to the hole, and he and Rigel between them somehow managed to stuff me through it.

I lost consciousness again. I just remember Betelgeuse saying, 'I'll go ahead on the lifeline. I don't think there's any time to lose.'

I kept swimming in and out of consciousness as Rigel helped me along the lifeline, which he had left to guide us back through the ship to the flight deck, rather like Ariadne's thread. Betelgeuse appeared to have vanished ahead of us. The journey was difficult because of my physical condition and awkward because the intercom was no longer working.

After what seemed an endless procession of hatches and ladders we arrived at last on the flight deck. Back home, as it were. Betelgeuse was already out of his suit, a great grin on his red face. He energetically began to help me. 'That was a close call, my friend. It will never be nearer than that,' I heard him say as he opened up my helmet.

'Not until it really is the end,' I replied with a weak smile.

'We're a long way from that, thank goodness.'

'Where is Alcyone?' I asked. There was just Betelgeuse, Rigel and myself there on the flight deck. By way of reply, Betelgeuse pointed towards Rigel.

'That is Alcyone!' he exclaimed, to my astonishment.

A moment or two later I saw this to be correct, for Alcyone's rich auburn hair appeared as she removed the helmet.

'Dick, we couldn't make your intercom work when we changed your support pack,' she began, 'so I couldn't let you know it was me.'

She flung her arms around me and we held each other for a long moment.

'But where did the life-support pack come from?' I asked.

'I brought one with me. I thought you might be in trouble. You see, I'd given up hope of your ever getting back again.' There were tears in her eyes. As I held her again, I caught sight of Betelgeuse. He was pretending to occupy himself at the console desk. So Alcyone must have handed the spare support pack out through the hole she had made with the cutting tool, and Betelgeuse must have contrived to change my worn-out pack for the new one. In two to three minutes. He must have done all this knowing that his own support pack was likely to give out at any moment. Yet he had waited there for me to revive. He had helped me in through the hole, before making his way to safety along the lifeline.

'But where is Rigel?' I asked.

'Rigel was hurt, when the torpedoes went off,' answered Alcyone. 'Either the Yela must have fired the torpedoes or there was a mistake somewhere in the electrical controls. Rigel may be able to tell you – later.'

'How badly is he hurt?'

'It was a big electric shock, with some burns. The re-action was very serious, but the main danger is past. He will recover.'

Betelgeuse turned from the console. 'Rigel is in what we call the "between-land".'

'Between consciousness and unconsciousness?'

'More between sleep and unconsciousness.' He came across and took Alcyone by the shoulders. 'It was well done,' he said decisively, 'to look after Rigel so well, and then to put out the wire.'

'It seemed the only way I could find out if you were alive.' Alcyone brushed the tears from her eyes.

Then Betelgeuse turned to me. 'Alcyone did very well,' he repeated. 'She is not an engineer, but she cut a way out through the skin of the ship as well as any engineer.'

He might have added that she also remembered the

spare support pack, which an engineer might not have done. Then he shook his head gravely and said in a deep bass voice, 'With Rigel also alive we have been lucky. Very lucky.' Objectively, this was a strange statement, since we were imprisoned in the ship, which was now a captive of the Yela. But subjectively I knew exactly what Betelgeuse meant. I knew there would be no more lighthearted fixing of hawsers, no more lighthearted firing of torpedoes. From here on we would proceed with the greatest caution.

'Has there been any trouble with the main life-support system?'

'No, everything has continued to function,' answered Alcyone.

'The nuclear generator is operative,' said Betelgeuse, pointing to the console desk.

'What happened when the first Yela exploded?'

'Was that what happened?' Alcyone exclaimed.

'Didn't you see it on the monitor?'

'The monitor became a malfunction after the misfiring of the torpedoes.'

I explained about the lances of fire that had crossed the sky, moving along the tracks of the torpedoes, of how the fire had raced along the hawser, and of how the Yela had exploded in a vast ball of flame.

'Surely something happened here in the ship,' I went on. 'We could see the ship in a huge corona of light.'

'For a moment my hair stood completely on end.'

'That would mean a change in the interior electric potential. The light must all have been on the outside.'

Alcyone went over to our space suits, which she examined with great care.

'Looking for something?' I asked.

'Perhaps.' She smiled. 'But Dick, there are still many things that puzzle me. Why did you not come straight to the ship? I could hear your voices on the radio for such a long time. You seemed just to be going round and around, without any purpose. Was there something wrong with the jet packs?'

'Of course Alcyone does not know about the second Yela,' broke in Betelgeuse.

'The second Yela! I think you had better tell me everything from the beginning.'

'Dick will do that, while I take a look at Rigel. Are the medical instruments working?'

'The nerve-system electrogram is working.'

'Good, that is the important thing.'

So Betelgeuse left me to tell as best I could the story of our exploits, from the moment the recoil from the firing of the torpedoes had shaken us loose from the ship. Alcyone became particularly interested when I described the explosion of the Yela. At the end she walked once more over to our suits.

'What are you thinking?' I asked again.

'From what you have said, material from the Yela was scattered in all directions by the explosion. So some of it must have reached you.'

'Yes, it poured past us in a kind of diffuse river.'

'So some of it must have become impregnated in the material of the suits.'

I began to see what Alcyone was driving at. 'You think that by doing a chemical analysis of the suit you can find out what the Yela is made of.'

'Yes, the *inside* of the Yela,' Alcyone said.

'I expect you'll find copper and zinc and nickel and aluminium and oxygen and . . .'

'Oh, you are completely hopeless!' she exclaimed, gathering up the suits and stalking away with them.

I found some leaves, which I began to munch, after swallowing a bundle of concentrated pills. With Rigel out of action, I would have to take charge of the electronic side. Betelgeuse would be mostly concerned with the state of the engines and with the general space-worthiness of the ship itself. The wire outside the ship would be picking up a great deal of data, from the stream that was flowing between the Yela's sensory devices and the sphere itself. All the data, whether optical, infrared, or X-ray, would have some form of radiotelemetry. I wondered if it would be possible for us to decode any part of it. Perhaps in this way we might be able to replace the monitors that we had lost. I decided to have a long sleep before tackling what I knew would be a difficult and extensive task. While I was making up my bunk Betelgeuse returned.

'How's Rigel?' I asked.

'He will recover, but it will be quite a while before he's back to normal.'

'Is the computer working, by the way?'

'It seems to be. Why?'

'We shall need it.'

'I don't see why particularly. The ship is totally inoperative,' grunted Betelgeuse.

'We shall see,' I said as I stretched out luxuriously on one of the bunks.

'What d'you mean by that?'

I was too tired to reply. All I could think of was that it would be a long time before Betelgeuse would get me outside the ship again. I would have been astonished to be told that the next time I would leave the ship would be to set foot on the Earth. And I would have been even more astonished to learn of the manner in which we would reach the Earth, now more distant than a hundred light-years. Within a couple of minutes I was asleep.

12 Out of the Galaxy into Deepest Space

Alcyone took both suits to a well-equipped laboratory. Since enough spare suits were available, she did not hesitate to cut off convenient-sized pieces – to begin with, about a foot square. One of these she cut into still smaller pieces. The rest were put away in storage in a low-temperature freezer. Dressed now in decontaminated clothing she first examined a specimen under the microscope. Another specimen went into a centrifuge. Meanwhile she made trial tests on a high-resolution magnetic spectrograph to make certain that it was fully operative. When altogether satisfied she turned her attention to a powerful but compact furnace. The first step in her analysis would be to obtain a series of flame spectra at a variety of temperatures. Oddly enough she left perhaps the simplest part of the preparatory phase to the last. What she had done with the suits that Betelgeuse and I had worn she did with a brand new suit. With reluctance she cut it into similar-sized pieces, carefully labelling them as she proceeded. These would be required for comparison purposes. It offended her sense of space economy to destroy a perfectly good suit, being fully aware of what such a suit could mean in a crisis – what even a spare oxygen cylinder could mean.

Betelgeuse had plenty to occupy himself. Having assured himself that Rigel was 'as well as could be expected', he began a tour of inspection of the ship. The first priority was the engine, the ION engine which was his pride and joy. From the console on the flight deck he checked the nuclear generator. This was certainly working, otherwise the main life-support system would have been unserviceable. Besides the digital monitors on the flight deck there were various analogue devices built into the engineering system. These had to be checked on the spot, which meant a complete tour of the ship. But before this could be carried out it was necessary to extend the life-support system everywhere through the ship. Since the Yela seemed to be no longer exerting any baleful influence on the operation of the automatic controls, there was no reason why this should not be done – except that Alcyone had cut a hole in the outer skin, through which air would instantly escape. The first job therefore was to put an airtight seal over the hole. While engaged on this job Betelgeuse also gave his attention to the crude wire antenna which Alcyone had so resourcefully managed to push outside the ship. Betelgeuse replaced it by a much more sophisticated arrangement, which gave automatic tuning at whatever frequency an operator on the flight deck might wish to choose. This modification was later to prove an enormous advantage to me.

With all this done, Betelgeuse at last began his tour of the ship. There were many details that did not meet with his approval, but nothing seemed fundamentally amiss. Mostly as he went about his examination he gave a series of grunts, which were relayed into Alcyone's laboratory on the ship's communication system. At first she paid no heed to them, but then with a wry grimace she cut the frequencies from 5kHz downwards so that the grunts became like little squeaks. After amusing herself this way for a while, she found even the squeaks to be an irritation, and so switched them out entirely. There was no point in telling Betelgeuse to shut up, for he must be very tired, she thought.

Betelgeuse was indeed near the point of exhaustion, but like all space people he drove himself to the limit as long as there was any question of the space-worthiness of his ship being involved. During his stay on Earth he had repeatedly slept through important political meetings. But he would not sleep now if anything remained to be checked that he thought should be checked.

When at last he decided to return to the flight deck he had a complete list of all the adjustments and modifications that he and, hopefully, Rigel would carry out in the days, weeks and months ahead – assuming that all went well, of course. There was still one crucially important thing to be done before he took some rest, to start up the ION engine itself. Unlike chemically fuelled engines, the ION system worked at low thrusts, up to one-tenth g, and at high jet speeds – which meant excellent efficiency. These engines were used for all interstellar purposes. They were also suitable for planetary landings, provided there was an atmosphere of sufficient density to give adequate frictional resistance to the motion of the ship. They could not be used for planetary takeoff, however, except for small planets, like Mars, with low surface gravity. For planets like the Earth it was necessary to make use for a short time at least of the chemically fuelled engines. These operated on a mixture of oxygen and hydrogen peroxide. Although from a terrestrial viewpoint this was a seemingly old-fashioned technology it had the important advantage that the fuel tanks could be topped up on any planet where there was water. Using nuclear power the oxygen and hydrogen peroxide were generated electrolytically, with power provided by the nuclear reactor. In this way the ship had an ongoing system, which would continue to be effective as long as the nuclear fuel lasted. Since the ship carried a very large store of enriched nuclear material, the functional capability was sufficient for very many human lifetimes. It was this whole system whose fundamentals it was now Betelgeuse's purpose to check.

Once he was satisfied that as much had been accomplished as was possible for the time being, Betelgeuse did what he had longed to do for a long time. He started the ION engine, at first at very low thrust and then with increasing drive. Nothing happened, except that at full power a slight tremor ran through the ship. The accelerometers showed absolutely no change in our motion. We were held by the Yela's magnetic field like a block of wood in a vice.

Yet some hours later, at about the time I awakened from my sleep, the accelerometers began to show a non-zero reading. This was due not to our engines, as Betelgeuse soon discovered, but to the Yela itself. As the hours passed by, the drive steadily increased. By now I watched the meters anxiously. Not that I needed to be told about the drive. From the considerable artificial weight we were assuming it was clear that the drive was strong. From one-third to a half g. Then to g itself, and still increasing. What was happening was that the ship, remaining trapped in the Yela's magnetic field, was being forced to accelerate as the Yela ship itself accelerated. There was no escaping this externally imposed drive. I began to fear that it might become so strong that we would be crushed by the pressure. The human body will stand up to three g, or even five g, but only for short lengths of time. Fortunately the drive levelled out at one-and-a-half g. This was like a 140-pound man finding himself weighing 215 pounds. It was unpleasant but tolerable. From here on, for the rest of our journey, this was what we had to put up with. It was just as if we had all suddenly become grossly overweight.

By the time I was fully awakened and ready to tackle our electronic problems, Betelgeuse was about all in.

'You need rest. Plenty of it,' I said.

'Bifusticator, but there is no untruth in that.'

'Satisfied?'

'Mostly so. But I will need an opinion from Rigel before I will be fully satisfied.'

'How is Rigel? I should have asked before.'

'Alcyone thinks he will be active again – well, in a few hundred hours.'

'Good, I will be needing help.'

'Decoding will be difficult.'

'The trouble is we have no idea what form of data is useful to the Yela, but I think some kind of geometrical picture of the world is probably necessary for all creatures. At any rate that's the idea I'm going to work on.'

Betelgeuse pressed his feet on the floor of the flight deck and flexed his knees, sensing the pressure. 'I just wonder where it is the Yela is going,' he murmured.

'Have you thought how lucky it is?'

'What?'

'That the ship fits into the Yela's magnetic field the way it does. We must be on a kind of equatorial plane.'

'How is that?'

'Otherwise the main axis of the ship wouldn't be in the direction of the Yela's motion, would it?'

Betelgeuse thought about this for a while. As I saw his eyes open wider I knew he'd spotted the point I was hinting about. If the acceleration had been across the line of the ship we should all have ended up in a heap at one side of the flight deck, for we would have had no means of compensating the component of force parallel to the floor beneath our feet. The situation then would have been worse than the most severe earthquake. The ship was constructed only to withstand large forces directed along its length. Betelgeuse stood there for a long time. Then he scratched his head, and simply said, 'You are right there, Dick. It is lucky.'

I made no further comment, so he went off for his well-earned rest. I reckoned he must have been more than two hundred hours without sleep.

I had already expressed in my remarks to Betelgeuse the basic difficulty in the task ahead of me. The problem was to discover the input code for the data that were being gathered by the Yela. I could expect our improvised antenna was picking up a formidable battery of radio signals. To put it crudely, the problem was to know what to do with them. If I simply put the signals through an ordinary amplifier onto a loudspeaker, say, the result would be an unintelligible stream of clicks and hisses. I wouldn't do any better if I put them onto a television screen. The result in that case would be no more intelligible than a television set with all its controls wildly out of adjustment.

At any rate the first thing to be done was comfortingly straightforward. This was simply to verify that signals really were being picked up by our antenna. Then I had to find out what kind of signals, what kind of pulses at what kind of pulse rates, what carrier frequencies were being used, what modulations. This information as it was disentangled was stored in our computer. Following this preliminary program the real work started. To search for regularities within the information. In effect this last stage was a kind of code-breaking operation, but it would have to be code breaking on a vast scale. It would be rather like trying to break a code when one had no idea at all of the language in which the original message was written. My idea of looking for a geometrical picture was in effect an attempt at guessing the language the Yela was using. If the Yela possessed geometrical concepts, then surely there must be such a picture. If there were not, how could the creature conceive of the positioning of its sensory devices? How could it conceive of a journey, or of where it was going? I was, of course, aware of the danger of over-emphasizing our human mode of thought, of supposing that *our* way was the *only* way. But in this matter of geometry I believed my supposition to be soundly based.

Alcyone brought news that was highly relevant to my problem, and very excited she was about it. 'You were wrong,' she exclaimed triumphantly.

'About what?'

'About there only being common metals.' She had evidently completed her analysis of the space-suit specimens, and had found something important.

'I suppose you want me to guess?' I said.

'I'll bet you can't.'

'Oh, you've found lots of carbon, and phosphorus, and nitrogen, and . . .' I knew from the disappointed look in her face that I was along the right lines.

'You know, biological material,' I concluded. 'Normal material. Contamination.' I thought this would be a disappointment. Nobody likes a hoped-for discovery to be downgraded into contamination. Not that I wanted to downgrade anything, but when one is called on 'to guess' there is always an implied challenge, a challenge to outwit the other person.

Instead of being in the least disappointed, Alcyone's eyes lit up brightly. 'Wrong! Wrong again!' she shouted triumphantly. 'It's not contamination!' she added.

So there was biological material there, I thought to myself. But how could she be so sure it wasn't simply contamination from life in the ship? There *must* be contamination, damn it. Contamination was absolutely unavoidable. Yet she was so sure of herself! There had to be a solution to the puzzle. What? I couldn't see any solution.

'I give up,' I said with a defeated smile.

'Write that down.'

'What?'

'That you give up. Then I can show you the bit of paper whenever you refuse to remember.'

So I wrote *I give up* on a bit of paper and handed it to her. Even now I had to wait for the relevant titbit of information.

'Well,' I said with impatience.

'Well,' she said slowly, 'well, the optical rotary properties are different – they're dextro.'

The brain is a singularly peculiar instrument. In most respects it operates very slowly, compared, say, to an inanimate computer. Yet in a few instances it acts with bewildering rapidity. The most obvious example is that of pattern recognition. Take a stack of many hundred photographs, all except one of persons unknown to you. Throw them down singly on to a table. How long does it take to recognize the known person from a horde of strangers? A mere fraction of a second. Using any procedure so far devised by mathematical experts, an inanimate computer would take very much longer.

So it was now, following Alcyone's remark. In only a fraction of a second a whole pattern of thought flashed clear in my mind. Biological material has the property of turning the plane of polarization of light. The material of which humans are composed always turns such a plane in a left-handed sense. This was true both for terrestrial humans and for the space people, because of our genetic relationship. It was true also of the plants on which we feed. Hence any contamination by biological material from the ship must have this left-handed property. It must be levo-rotatory, as the chemists say. What Alcyone was now telling me was that some of the biological material recovered from the space suits had the opposite property. It rotated the plane of polarization of light in a right-handed sense. It was dextro-rotatory. It therefore followed that this material could not have come from our ship. It had to come from the disintegrated Yela. Which meant that within the Yela sphere there was biological material, within the glittering orange metallic sphere there was a living creature. Absurd as the analogy might seem, I thought of an oyster living within its shell. Some oyster.

'I give in,' I said. I could have asked Alcyone for her proof of the dextro property, but that would have been a second-rate thing to do.

Alcyone must have seen the look of understanding flash across my face. She wasted no more time on argument, saying, 'I suppose this helps, doesn't it?'

'It means we're dealing with a living creature in the usual sense.'

'The Yela might have been one fantastic huge computer.'

'Of metal.'

'That's rather what you thought it was, didn't you?'

'I suppose I did. But why would a soft creature made more or less of the usual kind of polymerized biological molecules think in any different fashion than a computer made from hard metal?' I replied.

'I doubt if a computer can think at all!' exclaimed Alcyone, displaying womanly prejudice.

'You think there is a law of nature which requires a structure to possess molecules of a certain kind before it can be conscious, before it can think?'

Alcyone nodded and said gravely, 'Yes, it may be so.'

I shook my head. 'I doubt it. I doubt it very much. Yet this discovery certainly helps.'

'I don't follow you at all.'

'I mean it limits the range of possibilities. It limits the way in which the Yela operates. It limits it to the kind of things that are possible for biological creatures.'

'I still don't follow you. If you believe a metal computer can think for itself – well, where's the difference?'

'A metallic computer might have properties I can't conceive of – if its brain were superconducting, for instance. But with the Yela we know now that we're on familiar ground. It has the usual kind of brain. But god, what a brain – a thousand yards in diameter. No wonder the damn thing is able to outsmart us.'

'So how can you hope to understand what is going on in a brain as complicated as that?'

'Because we are not independent of each other, the Yela and ourselves,' I replied.

'How is that?'

'We both live in the same world. Which means that we're conditioned by the same physical circumstances.'

'You mean we have both evolved so as to cope with the same environment?'

'Not in a biological sense quite. But the same physical laws. Atoms and nuclei have the same properties for both of us. Electromagnetic radiation is the same. You know, a terrestrial creature called the octopus with a very primitive brain has almost exactly the same kind of eye as we do. Yet there's no direct relationship between the evolution of our eyes and the eye of the octopus. The two developed independently.'

'Yet they are the same?'

'The same in all essentials. The eye of the octopus is somewhat superior to ours in one or two details.'

'You say this is so because both have to cope with the same world?'

'Yes. Once a biological creature develops sight, in the sense of using light for the determination of geometrical images there is just one way to proceed. The way is the same because it is dictated by the basic physical laws. And it is the same whether the creature is low or high on the evolutionary scale.'

This was quite a mouthful and Alcyone pondered it for a while before replying. 'Yet the Yela doesn't have eyes in the usual sense. So it may be different,' she said.

'It won't be like the case of the octopus,' I agreed, 'but I'm hoping the reconstruction in the brain of the geometrical structure of the world will be the same.'

'If it is, you think you'll be able to use the Yela's own sensory devices.'

'Possibly. Otherwise it's going to be very frustrating, isn't it? Being simply pushed along in a blind ship, without the slightest idea of where we're going.'

'I think Betelgeuse would want to try placing some kind of optical device outside the ship.'

'Which wouldn't necessarily be a good idea.'

'Why not?'

'Partly because all the forces that are now operating on the ship are of a kind that none of us is used to.'

'We could become used to them.'

'Not if they were made stronger.'

'Stronger?'

'I'd imagine the magnetic field out there could be arranged to crush this ship just like a nut in a nutcracker.'

'What a horrible thought! If that's what you've got on your mind, I think I'll go straight back to work.'

'See if you can get some evidence of brain structure. It could be very useful.'

'Thank you for the hint. I'd have thought I'd been useful enough already.'

'You have. Particularly in reassuring me about the drive.'

'The drive?'

'Why it's limited itself at one-and-a-half g. Because one-and-a-half g happens to be the comfortable pressure for the biological creature inside that damned sphere. If we'd been dealing with a completely metallic creature it might have accelerated to ten g. Then we'd all have been wet smears on the floor.'

'Very comforting.'

'I was trying to be.' I grinned, shooing Alcyone back to her laboratory, for I was anxious to come to grips with the problems ahead. An idea for testing autocorrelations within the radio signals had occurred to me.

There is no point in describing at length the efforts of the following many hundreds of hours. There were many seeming breakthroughs which turned out to be only false starts. At no stage did it appear as though the ultimate objective was even remotely within sight. Yet there were always small successes, bits of correlations among the tangled information contained in the stream of radio signals, that served to buoy up my hopes. It was like trying to solve a huge multi-dimensional cryptic crossword puzzle. Total success seemed impossibly distant, yet every now and then an odd word or two fitted into place.

Alcyone, then Betelgeuse once he was rested again, and eventually Rigel after he emerged from convalescence were always on hand to give me an encouraging word whenever they judged it wise to interrupt me in the complex analytical work. I came more and more to discuss details with Rigel, who at one point made a suggestion that turned out to overcome a critical difficulty. After that I felt certain of a positive result, although how far success would go was still unclear.

The essential thing was to know what to reject. By now I knew that the sheer quantity of information contained in the radio signals was vast beyond precedent. In order to get something intelligible out of it I had to deal only with a part. Yet what part? What to reject, what to retain? The only system I could devise was to keep those bits that showed suitable autocorrelations. Even then I had to do a lot of trial and error before anything worthwhile emerged.

What I was looking for was a picture of the sky. Betelgeuse would have liked to try to reactivate the ship's own optical monitors, but I managed to persuade him to desist. Under the present strong drive any excursion outside the ship would have been exceedingly hazardous, quite apart from our lack of detailed knowledge of the form of the magnetic field in which we were trapped. Besides, the Yela's picture of the sky was likely to prove much superior to anything we could devise – if only we could find out how to make use of it.

As I have already said, it is not worthwhile describing all the false starts, the trials and the errors, by which I eventually got our first glimpse of the sky. It had a wildly unfamiliar look about it. There was no profusion of stars along the Milky Way, although there was some degree of concentration there. Except that I found a way of suppressing the brighter stars, but still keeping the fainter ones, and then the sky was quite uniformly covered. There was a general glow along the Milky Way, with an especially concentrated patch towards the centre. But there were similar, although less marked, patches in other parts of the sky.

'I think this is a picture in radio waves,' I said.

Rigel studied it for a while and then shook his head. 'I think not. These other bright patches, the ones not lying

162

in the plane of the galaxy, they wouldn't be present like this on a radio picture.'

'What d'you make of it then?'

'I think it is an X-ray picture. But I have never seen so many sources. The Yela must have very sensitive detectors.'

'And very directive,' I added. 'The resolution is remarkable.'

At this time Rigel had his head bandaged in a curious fashion. It gave him a kind of Gilbert and Sullivan appearance. I thought of referring to the *Pirates of Penzance* and then realized he wouldn't know what I was talking about.

Once the method of cracking the Yela's signals had been solved for X-rays, it was only a matter of time before we got pictures for other wavebands. As Rigel had said, the radio picture, while having superficial similarities to the X-ray one, lacked the notable bright patches outside of the Milky Way.

The picture we wanted to see most, the optical one for ordinary visible light, proved the hardest to obtain. Eventually we got it, but at first in a distorted projection. The Yela seemed to prefer not to use the simple human method of projection onto the celestial sphere. I found this so odd that I thought about it a great deal. I could only make sense out of the situation on the basis that the Yela was using some higher dimensional system of which our three spatial dimensions were but a part.

What we did to overcome this difficulty was to attempt actual star identifications. Provided our identifications were correct we could compare the known positions on our own system with those in the Yela's system. After a lot of agony and strife we found an exceedingly elegant mathematical relationship relating the two systems, although irritatingly it didn't fit exactly. At least this was the way it seemed to be at first. When the mathematical system was used to transform the Yela's representations it gave a visual picture, which we displayed on our monitors, a little different from what at first we had expected. Then I exclaimed, 'But the difference could be due to our motion. The stars are beginning to move towards our point of convergence again, just as they did before.'

Our point of convergence was of course the point of intersection of our direction of motion with the celestial sphere. The relativity effect was beginning again. We were finding it sooner than before because of the stronger drive we were now experiencing.

I chanced on a peculiar situation: a list of star positions in exactly the same code as the ones we were displaying with the aid of the optical monitor. The list was separate, however, and different. I was able to show it separately, simply by switching off the normal picture and by replacing it with the stars from this curiously isolated list. The question was: why this separation? Why arrange the stars into two distinct groups, one giving the main display and the other some special grouping? The special list had far fewer stars in it and they were mostly bright, implying that they were quite nearby. For a while I thought they might be stars with inhabited planetary systems, which would have made this special list immensely valuable. Then Rigel poured cold water on my attractive suggestion, by noticing that three of them coincided with the three stars that we ourselves had found to be missing, the three stars in the Ursa Major region, the three stars that had evaporated under mysterious circumstances. Evidently, then, the special list was not of stars but of *missing stars*. We were thoroughly astonished that there could be so many of them. How could all these stars have evaporated? I found myself developing the conviction that the answer to this question would somehow tell us a great deal about the Yela.

'Could the Yela be doing it?' asked Alcyone.

'I doubt it. This has to be something even bigger than the Yela. Exploding a planet is one thing, but a star . . .'

Alcyone cut me off with an excited wave of the hand. 'It

may bring us back to what you said once before. Perhaps the Yela is under some kind of attack,' she exclaimed.

'I've been trying to think what that would involve,' I said.

'What would what involve?' asked Betelgeuse coming towards us.

'Alcyone has raised the idea that the Yela might be under attack.'

'So?'

'I was trying to see what might be involved, especially in this business of evaporating stars.'

'It is difficult to understand that.'

'Damned difficult, but some kind of laser might be the answer.'

'Laser?'

'Yes. It looks to me as if a beam of cophased radiation lit up our torpedo tracks, out there. Then the beam exploded the Yela. Perhaps the same kind of thing was responsible for the missing stars.'

'How much energy would be needed?' asked Alcyone.

'To evaporate a star? Something like 10^{48} ergs.'

'That would be the energy going into the star,' grunted Betelgeuse. 'But how much energy would be needed at the source of your light beam, my friend?'

'It would depend on the dimension of the source of the beam, wouldn't it?'

'How would that be?' Betelgeuse was frowning and shaking his head in disbelief.

'Well, for the least energy requirement the cross-section of the beam would need to be no larger than the star itself?'

'I can see that.'

'Let's suppose the source of the beam happens to be somewhere on the opposite side of the galaxy, say 10^{22} centimetres away. The ratio given by dividing this distance by the radius of the star, say 10^{11} centimetres, would have to be not less than the dimension of the source of the beam

165

divided by the wavelength of light. Otherwise there would be a loss in efficiency.'

'I believe you, my friend. How big then would the source be?'

'With the numbers I've just given you, about ten kilometres.'

'Are you asking me to believe that somewhere in the galaxy there is a kind of lighthouse with a size of ten kilometres?'

'It comes out strikingly similar to the diameter of a neutron star.'

'But the light would need to be coherently phased across the whole ten kilometres,' continued Betelgeuse.

'Remembering the properties of a pulsar, the idea doesn't strike me as absolutely impossible,' I persisted.

'How much energy could there be in such a neutron star?' asked Alcyone.

'Plenty – if there were mass-to-energy conversion. Something like a million times more than would be needed.'

'To evaporate a normal star?'

'Yes, that's right.'

'But it would require such an object to have intelligence, to have purpose, to be *alive*, wouldn't it?'

'I don't see why life shouldn't be based on nuclear properties as well as on chemical properties,' I replied. 'It might be based on nuclear magnetic moments, shall we say.'

Betelgeuse was more serious now. 'This will bear much thinking about,' he said gravely.

'What other explanation do you have?'

'None, but my failure to find an explanation doesn't make yours correct, my friend.'

Alcyone was still very puzzled. 'How could such a creature, if it existed, ever come to be in a kind of war with the Yela?' she asked.

This was a new thought to me. 'Well, perhaps you might represent such a war as a clash between two intelligences each of the highest order in its own particular way, the

Yela being life based on atomic chemistry and this new thing being based on what we may call nuclear chemistry. A kind of clash of ultimate opposites.'

We thought about this for a while, all three of us. A new thought struck me. 'It might not be like war in the usual sense,' I stated.

'And what might you mean by that?' growled Betelgeuse.

'I mean it might not be the kind of emotional warfare we're used to in conflicts between one group of humans and another. It could arise more or less naturally, inevitably, as an interface between two life forms of basically different kinds.'

We left the matter at this point, none of us by any means convinced, but all of us thoughtful about the idea. As Betelgeuse had so aptly remarked, the absence of a satisfactory alternative did not require this particular theory to be right. Yet nothing else we could think of remotely fitted the facts.

Rigel was more concerned about hard facts than he was about theorizing on life forms in general. He kept a close watch on the information we were receiving from outside the ship. He was especially concerned about the direction in which the ship was being accelerated. He knew the direction of our motion from the relativistic point of convergence of the stars around us, and he knew from the fact that this direction stayed essentially the same that we were being persistently accelerated along this same line. We were not on a curved path but on a straight one. To where? The surprise was that our journey seemed to be taking us more or less perpendicular to the plane of the Milky Way. In other words we were headed out of our galaxy altogether.

This appeared to me most peculiar. It cast doubt on my theory, for if the Yela was concerned with a relentless enemy within the galaxy, it was strange it should now be headed entirely away from the galaxy. Unless we were started on a fantastic voyage of intergalactic migration. I pondered this question during much of the following hundreds of hours. I wondered if the Yela, faced by a superior intelligence, had decided to leave the galaxy altogether, in which case the chance of our ever returning to Earth must be considered impossibly remote. What then was there to do with the rest of our lives? I was beginning now to understand what Alcyone had meant when she had referred to survival as a religious issue. Only by giving the continuity of life a religious significance could we hope to preserve sanity.

13　The Quasar

Betelgeuse, like all engineers, was mightily pleased with himself whenever he sat down to a theoretical calculation. He had been figuring away with an intense look of extreme concentration, when suddenly he turned to the three of us, and said, 'It is hard to believe. If this strong acceleration maintains itself we shall be entirely outside the galaxy in little more time than it took to make the journey into Ursa Major. Only doubling the acceleration makes a huge difference in the distance one travels – in the same time, of course.'

I glanced at the sheets of paper on which he'd been working, to verify that he'd deduced the correct basic formula, which has a sinh dependence on the acceleration and on the time of travel.

'Yes,' I said, 'and you've only got to double the travel time and you'll find that we shall be at the far side of the universe – hundreds of millions of light-years away.'

'Assuming the acceleration is maintained?'

'Yes, assuming the acceleration is maintained,' I agreed.

Betelgeuse seized his working pad and began calculating again. After only a minute or two he looked up and stared wide-eyed into my face.

'Yes, Dick. You are quite right. It is entirely astonishing. We shall be hundreds of millions of light-years away. It is quite amazing.' With his face wreathed in smiles, he was entirely unaware of the grim implication of the facts, so engrossed was he in the work.

Alcyone came over to where we were standing. 'How is

it,' she asked, 'that all this relativity effect was not so important before?'

'Because our I O N engine gives a much smaller acceleration,' answered Betelgeuse, somewhat inaccurately.

'So it would have taken much longer to show,' I added, 'many human lifetimes.'

'Besides,' said Rigel, speaking from the control console, 'we were always changing the direction of our acceleration. The effect disappears when the direction of the acceleration is reversed.'

This conversation prepared us in only a modest degree for the events that followed. As they had done on our earlier journey, the stars moved more and more towards the point of convergence of our motion. This we expected. What we all misjudged, however, was the astonishing behaviour of our whole galaxy. Even when we verified by calculation that our observations agreed precisely with theory, we still could not accept the situation as being really believable.

To set the matter in perspective consider, first, what a traveller moving at a moderate speed, say a thousand kilometres per second, would observe as he quit the galaxy. If, as in our case, he moved away in a direction more or less perpendicular to the plane of the Milky Way, he would see a normal spiral galaxy oriented face-on. Because of its nearness the whole Milky Way system would fill a considerable fraction of the sky and would indeed present a magnificent spectacle, since it would appear about a hundred times brighter than the nearest other galaxy, the famous spiral in Andromeda – M31, to use the old catalogue designation.

Because of the persistent acceleration, we had attained a speed close to that of light by the time we quit the galaxy. This produced relativistic effects that were wildly different from the experience of our hypothetical low-speed traveller. It seemed only common sense to expect to observe things in the direction from which we had come –

this is what the low-speed traveller would find: the galaxy would be seen backwards towards the wake of the ship. But in our case we saw the galaxy *forwards,* and we saw it not as a spiral but as an intensely bright ring *centred on the direction to which we were heading.* At the stage where we were 'outside' the galaxy, in the sense of the low-speed traveller, the bright ring was only a few arc minutes in diameter. Over the rest of the sky there was nothing but a faint, very red glow. There was nothing detectable in the backward direction.

'I don't understand it all!' exclaimed Alcyone. 'If we have left the galaxy behind how can it be there in front of us?' She pointed at the bright compact circle displayed on our monitor screen.

'When you put it like that it is hard to explain,' grunted Betelgeuse, scratching his head.

He and Rigel had long arguments with Alcyone, trying to convince her that what we were finding was only right and proper. I took no part in these discussions, for I knew the only way to understand the things we were now observing was through the mathematical theory. Trying to argue in words was useless. I simply amused myself by increasing the confusion, by predicting even more outrageous things to come.

'You know, the galaxy will seem to get even more ahead of us the farther we go away from it – assuming the acceleration continues, of course,' I said.

'That is ridiculous. How can it get more ahead of us than it is now?' asked Alcyone.

'The bright circle will get smaller. The circle will close in more and more on its centre. And it will seem to get brighter, although the total amount of radiation from it will stay more or less the same.'

'I can see the circle will get smaller,' muttered Betelgeuse, 'but I would have thought it would gradually fade out as we get further out into deep space.'

'You'll find it won't. It'll seem to get brighter,' I re-iterated.

'Because of the blue-shift effect?'

'Where are all the other galaxies?' asked Rigel.

'The ones ahead of us are all inside the ring.'

'I suppose we don't see them because the contrast is too great.'

'That's right. The ones behind our galaxy are outside the ring and they're very faint.'

'What does that talk mean?' asked Alcyone.

'Well, if we tried to see other galaxies on the monitor, the ring due to our own galaxy would become impossibly bright – it would burn out the screen.'

'We might try some nonlinear saturation device,' suggested Rigel.

'That might be a good idea,' I agreed. 'Although eventually we *shall* see other galaxies. They're going to get brighter and brighter as time goes on. In fact eventually a lot of galaxies will become as bright as our own.'

'Those inside the ring?'

'Yes, those inside the ring. By that time the ring itself will be only a fraction of a second of arc in diameter,' I added.

'Which means we must find a different way of representing the picture. Otherwise it will become much too concentrated,' said Rigel thoughtfully.

'I've been thinking about that. My first idea was to set up a simple optical magnifier. But then we should be magnifying all the imperfections of the screen.'

'So we must do the magnification electronically, before reaching the screen.'

'Right again, Rigel. The trick is to find out how to do the electronics correctly. To keep the picture from becoming artificially distorted.'

Rigel considered this last point for a considerable time.

'That isn't going to be so easy,' he muttered.

'Nothing is easy,' said Alcyone, 'in this new fantastic

world. Here inside the ship everything is normal; yet out there everything is absurd and outrageous.'

Betelgeuse nodded and sucked in his breath. 'It is most curious, most curious. I wonder what it will all come to in the end,' he whispered, rocking gently on his heels.

I was delighted to find that the key to our problem lay in exactly the mathematical transformations I had used at an earlier stage, when I had changed the Yela's picture of the sky to the kind of picture we ourselves wanted to have. That is to say, the kind of picture we worked at first, before our speed of motion became so large. It turned out that by removing these transformations we immediately got something much more in line with our present requirements. In other words, the Yela's picture had seemed peculiar to us precisely because it was suited to relativistic motion. With very little extra modification, Rigel and I were able to display *our* galaxy, the galaxy we were now leaving behind us, as an apparently quite large ring. This became an equator, in such a way that objects in one hemisphere were almost entirely dark – these were objects behind our galaxy – while in the other hemisphere objects were much brighter. We referred to the two hemispheres as D and B. Our interest lay obviously in the bright hemisphere, the B hemisphere.

As the ship continued to accelerate, objects in the B hemisphere brightened to an amazing degree. These were the galaxies towards which we were now moving. Their wonderful patterns could be seen with startling clarity. We made a splendid tape record of this amazing and unique view of the world, recording the changes as they occurred.

While Rigel and I were working on our setup, of which we were exceedingly proud, Betelgeuse asked, 'How is your theory now, my friend?'

'Which one?'

'About the Yela, the motive for this journey.'

'You mean about the Yela being under attack?'

'Yes, about this being a form of scouting trip. How can that be? We're clearly heading entirely away from our own galaxy.'

'I've thought a lot about that particular point,' I said. 'Either my theory was wrong or it wasn't big enough.'

'Big enough!' exclaimed Alcyone, joining in the conversation.

'Yes, big enough. Our trouble is that we always tend to think on a limited scale, a scale that suits our theories and our own technology. There could well be enormously more amazing things in the universe.'

Betelgeuse rocked on his heels. 'You would look better doing that if you had a big cigar,' I added.

'Ah, yes, that would be good. But they are all finished.'

'It wouldn't be good at all,' said Alcyone crossly. 'They didn't do you the least bit of good.'

'I know by the look in your eye, my friend, that you have some new idea, working away in your head,' grunted Betelgeuse, ignoring Alcyone's interjection.

'Not a new idea at all. The same idea.'

'How could that be possible?'

'Well, the laser beam would need much more power. If it comes from outside our galaxy, I mean.'

'From outside the galaxy! That is a strange idea!'

Betelgeuse pawed the floor with his feet. Then he began striding backwards and forwards along the whole length of the flight deck. 'It is now that I need a cigar. If I am to keep calm,' he exclaimed at length. 'What manner of creature could operate from one galaxy to another, on an intergalactic scale?'

'It would need a power source at least a million times greater than we were thinking of before,' I answered. 'Even if the creature were operating from a nearby galaxy. To work a laser beam from a really distant galaxy – well, the power requirement would be much larger still.'

'I do not see how that could be.'

'Why not?'

'Before it needed something like a neutron star, to generate the power.'

'Yes, and now it needs something like a quasar.'

'A quasar! How could a quasar be phase-controlled?'

'I doubt whether the quasar itself would be phase-controlled. But the quasar might be the power source for a phase-controlled device.'

'Aha! So you think we may be on a scouting trip to some distant quasar – or to a creature who operates a quasar?'

'Something like that,' I nodded.

Betelgeuse began his pacing backwards and forwards again. Then he held up an arm in his characteristic dramatic gesture. 'So it is like this, is it? Although we shall never see our own people again . . .'

'Why should that be?' broke in Alcyone.

'Because of the time dilatation again,' I explained. 'Even if we manage to return, everybody on Earth, and everybody in your space fleet, will have aged by millions of years. Perhaps by hundreds of millions of years. In fact the human species will have evolved by that time into something else. Or become extinct!' I concluded, without too much enthusiasm.

'It is all this relativity. I do not like it,' Alcyone announced decisively.

'Although we shall never see our own people again,' continued Betelgeuse, raising his arm again, 'at least we shall see a quasar.'

'We shall see something even more remarkable than that. In fact Rigel is working on it right now. The beginning of all things.'

Rigel came up onto the flight deck at this point, carrying an armful of pieces of equipment. I helped him with them, while Betelgeuse and Alcyone came over and watched us plugging various electronic components into place.

'What d'you mean by the beginning of all things?' asked Alcyone.

'Well, one advantage of this relativistic motion is that it brightens galaxies ahead of us enormously. So we can now see galaxies farther away than we normally can.'

'Because normally they'd be too faint,' explained Rigel.

'I see,' nodded Alcyone. 'Well, at least that's one advantage of this peculiar relativity. How far can you see now?'

'We shall be able to see right to the beginning. The beginning of all the galaxies,' I answered.

'To see how everything was formed?'

'We hope so.'

'There is a practical difficulty,' Rigel explained again.

'Which is to distinguish farther objects from nearer ones, because the nearer galaxies have now become exceedingly bright.'

'Yes,' I added. 'Normally we have a problem of sensitivity. Now we have a problem of confusion. But Rigel is well on the way to solving it.'

This episode of the origin of galaxies and of the early history of the universe was to prove one of the most exciting and rewarding periods in our whole voyage. No terrestrial astronomer will ever be able to observe how things began in the fantastic detail that eventually was revealed to us. We saw masses of gas falling together to generate brilliant garlands of stars, which took on delicate patterns, mostly spirals, but with an apparently endless variety of subtle forms. Then there were violent explosions out of which came thousands of millions of stars. Once we had managed to exclude by a filtering process all the nearer more staid galaxies, we had a truly magnificent picture of the 'beginning' laid out before us. Although there might never be anyone to consult them, we taped a vast number of photographs and measurements of all kinds, and we documented all we had seen in satisfactory detail. The writing became a passion with me, for it occupied long hours of the voyage in a project that I found both exciting and deeply rewarding.

By now it had become clearer that the voyage was going to be a very distant one. According to the strange properties of the relativity theory, this meant we could estimate the subjective time taken by our journey to a fair precision, irrespective of the actual distance itself. Mathematically, this was because our time in the ship, the time measured on our clocks, the time determining our bodily metabolic processes, depended only logarithmically on the distance into space of our destination. For a distance into space of a million light-years our subjective time would be about ten years, while for a journey of a hundred million light-years the subjective time would be increased only quite moderately to fifteen years. Even for ten thousand million light-years – a journey across the universe itself – the subjective time would only be seventeen years or so. Since the nearest quasar was of the order of a hundred million light-years away, and since the farthest quasars would not be more distant than ten thousand million light-years, we therefore knew that the subjective time occupied by the journey would be somewhere in the range from fifteen to seventeen years – on the presumption, of course, that a quasar was to be our destination. Yet even if the purpose of the journey was to visit some object other than a quasar, the length of time we ourselves would experience could not be much different from this.

Alcyone had prepared a drug used by her people for circumstances precisely like this. It had the effect of reducing the metabolic rate, producing a kind of hibernation, which minimized the extent of the ageing process in the body. By using the drug it was possible to 'gain' in about a tenfold ratio. That is to say, for every ten years ticked away on our clocks in the ship we aged subjectively by about one year. Once we had satisfied ourselves that we had done all we were required to do, and all we wished to do, we began to make use of the drug, in order that the journey not consume too large a fraction of our lives. Betelgeuse waited before using it until he was satisfied that nothing could be done to improve further the mechanical condition of the ship. Rigel did likewise for the computer and for the electrical systems, while I waited until I had completed the work I have just referred to, and also until I had written an account to date of all our adventures. There was an important further reason for taking to a hibernation state. The sustained pressure to which we were being subjected amounted (as I have said before) to about one-and-a-half g. Indeed the subjective lengths of time given by our calculations were all based on this value of the acceleration. Besides being generally unpleasant, there was a continuing strain in having to experience constantly a fifty percent increase in 'weight'. It was not good from a medical point of view to be exposed to this strain for too long. Since in the hibernation state the ill effects were much reduced, it was important to spend as much of our time in this state as we reasonably could.

For the most part it was as if one were sunk in deep sleep. Yet from time to time we had to eat, and indeed the normal bodily processes still had to be attended to. It was just that everything went ten times more slowly, in a very, very sleepy way.

Then there was another point, a subtle one. A journey to a distant point, some hundreds of millions of light-years away, would occupy about fifteen years of ship time provided we accelerated continuously at one-and-a-half g for the whole journey. But suppose the Yela wished to slow down again in order to arrive at its destination with a low speed. Then after half the journey it would be necessary to replace acceleration by deceleration. Assuming a deceleration also of one-and-a-half g, nothing would seem to be changed. Yet the duration in ship's time for the deceleration would also be about fifteen years, the same as for the acceleration. Hence some thirty years would have elapsed in this case when the destination point was reached. So if there was to be a deceleration phase, the whole journey would take thirty years. This was too long to be contemplated in a normal ageing state. For this, hibernation was essential, which was true *a fortiori* if there was to be a return journey back to our own galaxy, since the return would also take thirty years. But for all we knew the Yela might decide to spend a great length of time, longer than our human lifetimes, at its destination.

Because a deceleration phase would double the time of the journey, we were naturally anxious to discover if there was to be such a phase. We knew that the switch from acceleration to deceleration would take place – if it occurred – after about fifteen years. With our use of Alcyone's drug this was metabolically equivalent to the passage of one and a half years. To the others this appeared an entirely acceptable duration, but to me it seemed appallingly long. However, in the hazy hibernation state one was hardly conscious of the passage of time, so I was not given to fretting about it. It was as if time simply rolled over us. I was vaguely aware that the fifteen-year stage was coming up and vaguely aware that important things were to be expected soon.

One day the supply of the drug, which I had become accustomed to taking in a routine way, suddenly wasn't there. The world still remained vague for many days yet, but without the drug my bodily processes gradually speeded up. My brain cleared of its perpetual fog and at last I was able to move about purposefully. There was still no change in the pressure. My normal 160-pound body still had an effective weight of 240 pounds.

I found Betelgeuse had 'wakened up' before me. It was he who had removed the drug.

'It is now T+140,000,' he said, 'and we are still accelerating.'

'Then we're well over a hundred million light-years into space,' I replied.

'Deceleration should be starting soon – if we're going to decelerate at all,' Betelgeuse grunted.

'We must. We must decelerate. What would be the point of the journey otherwise?'

'I don't know. That's why I thought you should be awake.'

I knew Betelgeuse had wakened me because he felt another full analysis of our external environment was necessary. By now all the relativity effects which we had encountered earlier would be further enhanced.

One glance at the monitor screen showed immediately what was worrying Betelgeuse. An intensely bright point of light shone out unwinkingly.

'That might be it,' I muttered.

'It certainly looks like a quasar. No structure to be seen.'

'That may be due to the light intensity. The damned thing is so bright. It may be suppressing something near-by.'

'Can it be filtered out?'

'That's what I'm going to try first thing.'

The problem of removing the quasar light was tricky, but once I had the idea for doing it the work didn't take long. With all the various adjustments made, Betelgeuse and I again took up position close to the monitor.

'Oroblatz! But there is something there, my friend.' Indeed there was. We could see a regular pattern of points of light surrounding the place where the quasar had been.

'And not natural either,' I said, in some triumph.

'I think the others should be awakened.'

'It would be a good idea. I've a feeling in my bones that something is going to happen – really happen – before too long.'

'How far away would you say the thing is?'

'I don't know. But we can find out.'

'How?'

'By measuring the rate at which its brightness is increasing.'

'Won't that take rather a long time?'

'Well, I calculate we must have travelled well over five thousand million light-years – from our galaxy. Staggering, isn't it?'

'I also get something like that. From $T+140,000$, and from the acceleration of course.'

'Fine. Well, let's suppose the quasar is still a hundred million light-years away. We shall reach it in something like 140,000 divided by fifty, 2,800 hours. A few months.'

'So in about a thousand hours it will increase quite a bit in brightness,' nodded Betelgeuse, deep in thought.

'Yes, but since we can measure very small changes in the brightness, it won't take anything like a thousand hours to come up with an answer.'

It didn't. By the time Alcyone and Rigel were fully awakened I had it. From the rate at which the quasar was brightening I knew the damned thing was between seventy and seventy-five million light-years away, and I knew we should reach it in less than two months. There was no more need for hibernation now. We all had plenty of work to do.

'How can we travel nearly a hundred million light-years in only a month or two?' asked Alcyone as soon as she was fully awake.

I explained as best I could about the Fitzgerald contraction. Our whole journey was thousands of millions of light-years in extent to a normal observer in a normal galaxy, but to us it was enormously less than this because of the contraction arising from our fantastic speed.

'If this quasar is our objective, why are we not decelerating now that we've almost reached it?'

'I just can't figure that one,' I replied.

'Perhaps we're going somewhere else?'

'Perhaps, but it seems rather unlikely. Because of those artificial patterns of light around the object.'

Rigel came across to us with an extremely puzzled look on his face.

'This is very strange,' he began.

'What?'

'The Yela is no longer there.'

'Perhaps it's behind us now, instead of in front. The way it was before.'

'No, it is not so. I would not be caught again by the same trick.'

Rigel was, of course, right. We checked his statement with the greatest care. Nowhere could we see the Yela ship.

Betelgeuse strode up and down the flight deck. 'Bifusticator!' he roared. 'The Yela has slipped off the hook.'

I forbore to point out that it was really we who had been slipped off the hook. It seemed clear that we must have come loose from the Yela's magnetic field during some deceleration manoeuvre, although why at this late stage the Yela should start deceleration was a mystery to me. It was far too late for deceleration – if the quasar was the objective, that is. Perhaps the quasar wasn't the objective?

Then in a flash the inconsistency struck me. 'But we're not weightless!' I shouted. '*The Yela must still be there.*'

The others instantly saw the point. The Yela must still be supplying the drive. The drive was much too strong to be due to our own ION engine.

'Switch on ship's lights,' thundered Betelgeuse.

Rigel quickly fed an appropriate program card into the computer. A moment later our lights picked up the Yela sphere, but only very faintly indeed. Astonishingly the shimmering metallic surface had gone. The sphere was now almost completely black, close to being a perfect absorber of light. Technically speaking, its albedo was somewhere in the 99.9 percent region – much, much blacker than coal. Nor was there any sheen on it. The exceedingly small amount of light that it reflected was being scattered more or less equally in all directions.

Our lights had not been on for more than a few seconds when over the loudspeakers of our intercom system there came a frenzy of electronic chatter such as I had never heard before. Several times we had encountered outbursts of this kind from the Yela but not with this volume or intensity.

'Sounds as though the bloody thing is having a brainstorm,' I muttered.

Rigel moved to cut the lights, but even as he did so a corresponding frenzy swept over the indicators of the console deck. A second later the lights failed throughout the ship.

'Not again. This is where we came in,' I muttered inaudibly.

We tried the fuses first, in the hope that whatever had happened was quite superficial. Certainly a great many had blown, but even after they had been replaced little of the ship's systems came back into operation. Starting the standby generator helped. At least it ensured that the life-support system became effective again.

Rigel returned from a tour of the whole ship and said, 'Much work will have to be done. I could not have believed so much damage could have been done in so short a time.'

There was nothing for it but to spend day after day replacing melted and damaged electrical components. We all lent a hand as best we could, although this was really Rigel's province. The nuisance of it, from my point of view, was that the circuits whereby we were analysing the signals from the Yela's own detectors had become inoperative. In fact the ship had become blind just at the most critical moment of our journey.

There was nothing for it but to work systematically, checking and repairing each section with care and with as little haste as possible. Our hope was that we would have spare circuits to replace all those that had been damaged. Our fear was that we would lack some vital card among our spares, some card which it would be impossibly complicated to build or rebuild by hand.

Alcyone and I were working on one of the simpler sections; we all preferred to leave the more complex parts to Rigel.

'What does it all mean?' she asked.

'What?'

'Oh, the darkening of the Yela ship. And all this . . .' She pointed at a charred segment of one of the main cables.

'If it didn't sound almost ridiculous, I'd say the Yela was trying to hide itself.'

'But from the point of view of the quasar aren't we still a very long way off?'

'Yes, perhaps millions of light-years.'

'Then why at such a distance would it be necessary to hide oneself?'

'From the point of view of a creature associated with the quasar we must seem like a projectile with fantastic energy,' I said, an idea forming vaguely in my mind. 'Remember that the beam from our searchlights, while seemingly of harmless light to us, would appear at the quasar as hard X-rays.'

'Could it conceivably be detectable?'

'At a distance of millions of light-years? It seems at first like a ridiculous idea, but not when one thinks about it a little more carefully.'

'How's that?'

'Well, I suppose the output *to us* would be about a megawatt. Remember the lights are very directive. To anybody staring straight into them – well, they would be like an isotropic radiator with more like a million megawatts. At a distance of ten million light-years the flux, for any creature looking directly into the light beam, would be what? I make it 10^{-35} watts per square metre per second.'

'Which is exceedingly minute.'

'Which would be 10^{-35} watts per square metre if we were not in motion,' I went on. 'But because of our relativistic motion this has to be multiplied by the square of the dilatation factor.'

'Why the square?'

'Once for the direct blue-shift effect and once for what is usually called the number effect – to allow for the difference between our clock rate and the quasar's clock rate.'

'So what d'you make it to come out in the end?'

'I make our present dilatation factor to be about 10^{10}. Multiplying by the square of this gives 10^{-15} watts per square metre per second. Yes, this could be detectable.'

'Our motion makes a fantastic difference!'

'Yes, enormous.'

'Then you think the Yela must deliberately have quenched our lights.'

'I'm fairly sure of it.'

'How?'

'Magnetically, I would think.'

'In what way?'

'Through induced currents. It's lucky only our electric system was affected. The Yela might simply have crushed us out of existence – like swatting a fly.'

A day eventually came when Rigel at last called a halt to our activities. 'I think we may have done enough,' he said.

We all made our way to the flight deck. With an air of ceremony Rigel and Betelgeuse began a systematic checking of the main operating program. As one set of circuits after another was found to be functional, a broad grin settled on Rigel's face.

'The exercise has been most useful,' he said with satisfaction.

'It gave me the chance to check almost everything more thoroughly than I'd done before.'

At last we came to the part I'd been waiting for, the quasar. Even with a very strong attenuation of the signals, the steely-blue unwinking object ahead of us was appallingly brilliant, appallingly menacing. Even during the time we'd spent on our repair work, the distance to the quasar had perceptibly decreased. We would reach it now in quite a short time. Our voyage was nearing its end.

'What is the point of it?' asked Alcyone.

'That is what I keep asking myself. It is strange, most strange. But then everything in our lives has become strange,' grunted Betelgeuse.

'The point of it all is very clear,' I announced. The vague idea I'd had before was now much better formed. I knew at last the motive of our journey.

'I think you had better explain, my friend.'

'The important question to ask oneself is why we are not slowing down. Why no deceleration.'

'I ask myself that a thousand times!' exclaimed Betelgeuse in exasperation.

'My old idea was that the Yela . . .'

'Was making a scouting trip. Yes, we know that, my friend.' Betelgeuse sucked in his breath and rocked on his heels.

'But that just can't be right. If we were on a scouting trip I think it would have been essential to slow down. Besides getting a longer view of the creature associated with the quasar – the creature deriving its energy from the quasar, I mean – besides that, we should be much less visible if we were to slow down.'

'Less visible because the dilatation factor would be reduced.'

'Right. No scout would approach its objective at the speed we're doing now.'

'So what d'you make of it?'

'We're not scouting. We're attacking,' I exclaimed – at last with commendable brevity.

'Attacking! Aha, there is a new idea! You never lack for new ideas, my friend.'

'The Yela ship is now a colossally energetic projectile,' I went on. 'It is going to enter the quasar system quite shortly – in three or four hundred hours, according to my estimates – and it is going to launch itself in a direct attack on the vital components of the creature there. This is the Yela's response to the laser beam.'

'The laser beam might be used to evaporate both the Yela and ourselves,' broke in Rigel.

'It might, and that was exactly why the Yela was so concerned not to be detected.'

'At any moment we might be destroyed. Just because we switched on the ship's lights!' exclaimed Alcyone.

'I'm not sure now. I think the main danger may be passed.'

'How is that?' muttered Betelgeuse.

'Looking at things from the point of view of this new creature . . .'

'Assuming there is one.'

'Yes, assuming there is one. Looking at things that way, it would not be an advantage to attempt to destroy us at a late stage. While we are quite compact, as we are now, there's a good chance of us doing very little damage. But if we were evaporated into a much larger cloud some part of us would be sure to hit vital parts of the creature's system. Just like the difference, in the old-style terrestrial weapons, between the iron cannonball and the high-explosive shell.'

'Perhaps it is the Yela's intention to explode itself!' suggested Rigel.

This was a new idea to me, and a likely one. The Yela might well be on a mission like those of the old-time suicide pilots.

We did not have much time to ponder these thoughts however. We were moving now into the radiation field of the quasar. This field was made vastly more intensive by our huge dilatation factor. In fact, the Yela would hardly need to explode itself. Evaporation would occur soon enough in any case. It did, with an unexpected suddenness. I had thought the ship's temperature control would gradually fail, probably over several hours, during which time conditions inside the ship would change inexorably from hot, to stifling, to insupportable for life, and finally to disintegration. Instead we passed instantly from a wholly comfortable condition to a luminescence which spread everywhere in a flash throughout the ship. My consciousness passed from a complete awareness into – nothing.

14 Transfiguration

First there was nothing. Then we were all there again on the flight deck. My memory of the events as I have just recorded them was vague, as if it had all been a dream.

Betelgeuse flicked a switch on the console. 'This is blue leader. Hello, Earth, are you reading me? Over.'

It was just as it had been after our takeoff from Earth, as it had been in the beginning.

'Where are we?' I gasped.

'Twenty hours out from Earth,' answered Rigel.

'Then I have just had a most peculiar dream,' I said.

'A dream? I thought you were sleeping soundly,' Alcyone remarked.

'I'd like to tell you about it. Before I forget.'

'Later,' grunted Betelgeuse, 'when I've set up contact with both Earth and with our fleet.'

I waited. Betelgeuse repeated his message, but there was still no reply.

'There must be a malfunction somewhere,' stated Rigel. Just as there was in my dream, I thought. Perhaps we were now locked into some existence that went round and round like a continuous tape.

'Better carry out routine checks,' Betelgeuse requested.

Rigel proceeded to run various tape decks into the computer. Eventually he shook his head. 'Our systems still seem to be working, but still no reply.'

'A malfunction at W.S.H.Q. then.' Betelgeuse characteristically began rocking on his heels.

'Which is peculiar,' I broke in. 'Perhaps I'd better tell you about my dream.'

Betelgeuse grinned. 'Perhaps you had. It will occupy the time while Earth repairs the malfunction.'

My memory at that stage was not at all precise, so my account of what I thought had happened was a lot vaguer and much shorter than the narrative set out in the preceding pages. Betelgeuse grinned and rocked on his heels throughout most of my recital, which tended to make me self-conscious about it. When both Rigel and Alcyone began to laugh more or less openly, I found it genuinely difficult to continue.

'Space dreams,' chuckled Betelgeuse when I had somehow managed to finish. 'I've never heard one quite as complicated as that,' he added.

'I liked the part about the relativity dilatation,' said Rigel.

'I didn't understand it at all,' remarked Alcyone.

'You didn't?' I mused. 'Which is interesting.'

'Why?'

'Just like in the dream. You found the same difficulty.'

I glanced over the console and added somewhat viciously, 'You don't seem to be getting much in the way of a reply to your signal, do you?'

'It's certainly taking time to repair the malfunction.'

'There's no reply for a good and solid reason,' I asserted doggedly, 'because we're a full billion light-years away from Earth.'

'Gallfinder! You believe it, then!'

'The dream must have been unusually vivid,' said Alcyone mildly.

'We'll soon settle the matter,' roared Betelgeuse. 'Rigel, run out the telescopes.'

Lights flashed on the console. Eventually the flickering stopped, to be replaced by a single steady red light.

'Another malfunction. Strange, isn't it?' It was now my turn to do the grinning. Although my memories were still very imprecise I was beginning now to give them real credence. 'Suppose you check on the malfunction,' I added.

'I'll do just that,' muttered Rigel, leaving the flight deck.

While he was away I went into a reflective, incommunicative mood, trying to dig deep into my memory, trying to clarify a whole host of still obscure points.

When Rigel returned I knew from the deep frown on his face that he had run headlong into something very unexpected.

'The airlock has gone!' he exclaimed.

Instead of becoming excited, Betelgeuse stared fixedly at me for a long time. Eventually he shook his head gravely. 'Mm. This is most strange. I am wondering if there can be something in what you are saying, my friend.'

'I think we've all experienced something akin to a physical accident,' I replied, 'the sort of accident where one usually suffers from a loss of memory. For some reason this just happens to be less complete in my case than in yours.'

'Except that it is impossible to be evaporated and yet to be alive,' broke in Alcyone.

'You would think so,' I agreed.

'Well, let us go to the place where Alcyone is supposed to have cut a hole in the skin of the ship,' suggested Betelgeuse, raising an arm in his most commanding gesture.

Even as we made our way to the rear of the ship I realized a discrepancy. We were neither weightless nor were we suffering from the fierce pressure which I believed we experienced throughout our long journey from the galaxy. The pressure was gentle, as was to be expected from the operation of our own ION engine. This did not seem to fit my picture of what had happened. Yet when we reached the rear of the ship there was the patch which Alcyone had cut on the occasion when she had saved my life. From the expression now on her face I could see that the chords of her memory were at last being struck. And in the same instant an obvious point clarified in my mind. It flashed suddenly out of the fog of oblivion like a welcoming beacon.

'We made a record of it all!' I exclaimed. 'It must be all there, stored among the tape cassettes.'

So we returned immediately to the flight deck. Deliberately without conscious thought, I went to the storage unit and tried to make my choice of tapes by instinct. Then the obvious point occurred to me that the tapes must all be labelled. Within half an hour we had verified on our monitor screens the substantial accuracy of my story. There once again were the astonishing galactic forms, going back in time to the very beginning of all things.

The others just had to be convinced now, and as conviction grew on them so flashes of memory began to occur also in their minds.

'What can it mean?' asked Alcyone in a plaintive and almost frightened voice.

'It can only mean something very strange and peculiar,' was the best answer I could offer.

'But are we *dead*?'

'I do not feel in the least bit dead,' grunted Betelgeuse. 'We shall achieve nothing by speculating, my friends. We need data. We must find out what lies outside the ship. It is intolerable to be trapped inside here.'

'It will be easy to open up the skin of the ship. We can unseal the patch at the rear,' nodded Rigel.

'Remember there may be floods of hard X-rays out there – because of our relativistic motion,' I pointed out.

'We can take good care of that. By using a periscope,' was Rigel's reply.

So back again to the rear of the ship. Rigel was as good as his word. Within a short time he had a crude optical periscope in operation. And now it was my turn to have my idea overturned. Instead of the picture we had just been examining on our tapes, the relativistic picture of the extra-galactic world, the sky was dotted with a profusion of stars. It was the picture to be expected by a low-velocity observer situated inside a normal galaxy.

Of necessity, we were wearing our space suits as we opened up the patch to the external world. Since we seemed to be in an ordinary low-velocity situation, not a relativistic regime at all, there was no good reason why we should not simply go outside into space ourselves, instead of bothering with the periscope. The radioactive monitors we'd brought with us showed no unusual activity. Nor was there any flood of X-rays. It should be safe, therefore, to clamber outside, provided we were careful with our lifelines and provided we took magnetic grips along with us.

The view that met my eye as I looked around this new world defied all explanations. First, the quasar had gone. Second, the Yela had gone. Third, we were in some galaxy of a more or less normal type. There was a concentration of stars along a plane, pretty much like the Milky Way. Stars dotted the rest of the sky, not in any recognizable constellations. Questions poured through my head. Where was the quasar? Where was the Yela? Where were we? To mention only the most obvious.

I say there was no quasar, but one star outshone all the rest at least a hundredfold. Yet this object was yellow, not blue like a quasar. Evidently we just happened to be much closer to one particular star than to any of the others. After we returned inside, Rigel managed to set up a more ambitious monitoring system, using small telescopes that he found in the ship's store. Once again we had a more or less normal display of the external world on our optical monitor. In fact our situation was normal in almost all respects – except that the skin of the ship was smooth everywhere. It was fused, as I remembered it to have been.

Rigel set about measuring the characteristics of the stars, as he had done once before. I left him to it, for I knew it would be a useless exercise unless we just happened to be back in our own galaxy among the stars which had been carefully catalogued in the past. Since there were no recognizable constellations to be seen, I did not think this at all likely. The idea of these star measurements was to make a comparison between what one observes and what has already been catalogued. Every star has small distinguishing characteristics. Like humans, no two are exactly alike. And of course once one has distinguished a few stars one knows where one is located – the method provides a way to fix position in space. But the method works only among known stars, as I have just mentioned. In a strange galaxy, among hitherto unobserved stars, it would not be helpful.

Once again I was wrong. Rigel suddenly raced across to where Betelgeuse and I were standing by the control console. 'It's the Sun!' he burst out.

'What is the Sun?' I asked, feeling quite shattered.

'The bright yellow star!'

'The near one?'

'Yes, the near one. It is easily within our range.'

'How far?' asked Betelgeuse.

'Several thousand hours. I can't say exactly, until my calculations are finished.'

I could see Rigel's estimate was approximately right. The Sun – if it *was* the Sun – could not be more than a tenth of a light-year away. This was clear from its brightness. Our ION engine gave an acceleration of about one-tenth g. About 5,000 hours was my own quick answer. If it *was* the Sun!

I asked Rigel to show me his results. I made a comparison of the spectrum of this nearby yellow star with the catalogue spectrum of the Sun. There was just no room for doubt. To within the errors of observation they were identical.

'You don't look too happy about it, Dick,' said Betelgeuse, coming up to where I was standing.

'There were no recognizable constellations,' I replied.

'I wouldn't expect any. After the journey we made. So far as the galaxy is concerned time must have run along for many millions of years. The stars should have moved and the constellations should be different.'

Alcyone came towards us and nodded at Betelgeuse's conclusion. 'That is the effect of this relativity dilatation, isn't it?'

I shook my head. 'The effect is too big. After a journey like ours the galaxy should be at least a billion years older.'

'Because we travelled at least a billion light-years?'

'Right. To an observer here in the galaxy we travelled at nearly the speed of light, so the elapsed time must have been something of that order.'

'Which explains why no constellations are to be recognized. The stars have moved. The galaxy has changed. It has rotated around many times.'

'It would certainly do that. But in a thousand million years the Sun would change too. Its internal evolution would change both the luminosity and radius. The spectrum would change . . .'

'Aha!' Betelgeuse interrupted, rocking once more on his heels. 'I see now what it is that is troubling you. Nothing fits.'

'That's right. Nothing fits. Nothing at all.'

'Mm. It is strange. Everything is strange.'

With this pronouncement I agreed most heartily. Throughout our journey from the galaxy many peculiar things had happened, things at the boundary of my understanding – and beyond. But I had always felt them to be within the range of rational understanding. The situation now seemed to go quite outside anything that was conceivably explicable.

The months that followed did nothing to clear up these mysteries. The Sun grew brighter, at first slowly, then more and more rapidly. We made great improvements in our techniques of observation. With the influence of the Yela removed, this had now become a fairly normal space voyage, except that we had to improvise our detection equipment.

As the Sun grew brighter, the belief that we were indeed approaching the solar system grew stronger within me. This conviction became a certainty once we were close enough to detect our planets – Jupiter first, then Saturn with its characteristic ring structure. There was no room for doubt.

The day came when we had our first view of the Earth.

'The elapsed time down there can't have been more than a hundred million years,' I said.

'How d'you know that?' asked Rigel.

'From the pattern of continents and oceans. It all seems to be essentially the same as it was. The characteristic time for change would be about a hundred million years.'

'I see.'

'I wonder how life has changed,' said Alcyone.

This was a topic I hardly dared to think about, for even a few thousand years must have produced enormous differences from the world of our departure. For better or for worse? This was a question that could only be answered after we landed. Where? W.S.H Q. in Baja California?

Just as the Sun had grown brighter as we neared the solar system, so the Earth now brightened and became ever larger on our monitor screen. It was the same blue sphere with the same swirling cloud structure that I had known from childhood. Delicate pastel colours began to appear. From these colours, and of course from the spectrum, we knew that plant life still flourished. The Earth had not become a sterile planet.

With a startling suddenness we were there, in close orbit around the Earth. Although it was not the home of the other three, I could see they were glad to be back. Perhaps more glad than I was. They would have hopes of news of their space fleet, while I was thoroughly tormented by fears of the disasters we might find down there.

We had much to do before moving in to land, so that we were content to orbit many times. Particularly we had to make emergency arrangements for reaching the ground.

Luckily Alcyone's impromptu exit was at the rear of the ship and so would be low down after landing. Rigel had no real difficulty in making the necessary equipment but it took him some time to do so. I spent many of these last hours of our journey at the monitor screen, searching for signs of human life. I could find none. There were no large cities of the kind I had known before, otherwise I would have seen their lights on the dark side of the planet.

Although after the vicissitudes it had passed through the ship was by no means in a normal condition, the landing presented little difficulty to a captain of Betelgeuse's experience. Instead of Baja California we chose the steppe country of Russia – of what had once been Russia, for I had no doubt that the political rivalries and ideologies of my own time were now only a small part of the forgotten past. We chose the steppe country because it looked green and invitingly flat, and because a nearby river would supply water for recharging our chemical fuel system. One of our first tasks after landing would be to prepare for immediate takeoff. This was a basic rule for Betelgeuse. He did not regard any planet as 'home'. To him a planet was a place where one recharged and restocked the ship.

Rigel was proud of his improvised landing system. We squeezed one-by-one through Alcyone's door and made our way about a hundred and fifty feet down the improvised steps to the ground. It was mightily strange to feel ground, real ground, under my feet again, to feel the wind on my cheek. Alcyone had once said that Earth people had no true conception of how lucky they were. I knew now exactly what she meant. In my exuberance I could have rolled on my back and kicked my legs in the air like a horse.

We strolled several hundred yards away from the ship. Rigel suddenly gripped my arm. A band of horsemen was sweeping over a small eminence about a mile away. We would just about have had sufficient time to run helter-skelter back to the ship. Although unanimously we decided against such an ignominious retreat, we prudently returned some way to the ship. It stood there behind our backs rearing like a vast monolith into the sky.

The horsemen came to a halt about fifty yards away. They were in line abreast, about two hundred of them, more than we could cope with, since we were unarmed. But we had brought several signal rocket devices down from the ship. It was a fair presumption that a flare from one of these would scare the horses, should an ugly incident develop.

I say 'horses', but really the animals were quite small ponies. The men were armed with leather headdresses, shields and jackets, with bows about two feet long and with small, rather ineffective-looking swords. They were all sharp in feature. I will not say that particular individuals of my own day were not somewhat like this, but I had never before seen such an array of small pointed noses, small pointed chins, and small unblinking eyes. Just like a row of mice, I thought. In the excitement of the moment I couldn't place what it was that was really wrong, however. It was only when they all simultaneously dismounted, with an almost military precision, removed their head-pieces, and bowed down before us – gods from the sky – that I knew what it was. They were hairless, without eyebrows. Every man-jack was totally bald.

At this stage it will be convenient if I pass from narrative style to more or less an essay form, since I intend to end this manuscript more with an account of the state of my thinking than by a further chronicling of events.

Through the nineteenth century and most of the twentieth century nobody seriously questioned the proposition that both technical and sociological progress would continue indefinitely. Even those few who thought much about these problems never fully understood the gravity of the situation that confronted the human species. Imagine a set of planets distributed through the galaxy, each suited to the development of life. Imagine the primitive beginnings, followed by a gradual development of more and more complex life forms. Imagine the eventual emergence of intelligent creatures capable of both emotion and reason. Each planet provides an opportunity for its creatures to rise from a crude struggle for life to a higher and more stable plane of development, from the pitiless cut and thrust of the jungle to the world of the late Beethoven quartets. But the opportunity is fleeting. A crucial point is reached where opportunities lie open for only a few generations. In the case of the Earth only from about A.D. 1800 to 2000. No longer than that. Before A.D. 1800 the situation was still too underdeveloped. By A.D. 2000 the development had proceeded much too far along a wrong road, a road in which giant world populations sought to live on ever-dwindling resources.

After the inevitable collapse nothing remained but a return to the jungle. No further climb, no development was possible. With resources consumed and with technology destroyed, no return to the former state, no recovery of past glories, could take place. Human beings divided themselves once again into tribes. Once again life became an endless feuding between one tribe and another, an endless progression of meaningless battles. Human culture became dedicated to survival at a trivial level. As the noses and chins of the people became small and sharp, the culture became cruel and meagre in its content.

Our arrival had been seen, by the particular tribe amongst which we happened to land, as an immediate divine intervention. We became *their* gods – in Alcyone's case, the star goddess from the sky. Their culture demands that we assert ourselves over the gods of neighbouring tribes, which of course we can easily do. In this way we would have no difficulty in making our influence spread out in wider and wider circles. Already human sacrifices in our honour have become widespread.

But to return to more general matters. Among our set

of planets in the galaxy there are very few that succeed in escaping permanently from crude savagery. Very few break through to a stable higher level. Only for a fleeting moment, as in the terrestrial period from A.D. 1800 to 2000, does a glimpse emerge of what might have been. The fate of the majority of planets is to reach a barrier which cannot be crossed. Life simply remains fossilized as in a galactic zoo. All this I have come to realize, partly from what I have learned following our landing and partly from much reading in the library of Betelgeuse and his space people.

The big question before us is what policy we are to follow. I have briefly mentioned before that our party is biologically sterile, so there is no possibility of starting a long-term program for repopulating the planet. It is not we who will survive genetically.

There appear to be just three possibilities before us. We could take off again in our ship and proceed to live out the rest of our lives simply travelling through space. The trouble with this course is that it would be one of profound anticlimax. Rejecting this first possibility then, if we are to remain here the essential issue becomes one of culture. Are we to descend to the level of these sharp-chinned little people, accepting the godlike roles in which they have cast us? Or are we to attempt to impress our culture on them? To succeed in this second possibility it will be necessary to attempt the long climb back to a developed society. It is by no means certain that we can succeed in this, although our technology, surviving in the ship, is strong. By a judicious use of the hibernation drug we might well be able to extend our influence and control for perhaps two centuries and would at least have a quite fair chance of success. The trouble here is that none of us feels an empathy (to use a word dredged up from the dim distant past) with these wretched people. They seem devoid of human values, which we ourselves are conditioned to admire. Nevertheless, I think this is what we shall decide to do. Our reason will not be concern with the people here. Rather does it arise from a deep underlying belief of Betelgeuse, Alcyone and Rigel that *their* people have continued to survive. We shall try to make something of this planet because someday the space people may arrive here again.

This gives a full and adequate motive for the other three. For myself? For myself, I am willing to accept a majority decision. Besides I am myself more concerned with the physical mysteries remaining from our voyage than I am with these cultural questions, and it is about the physical mysteries that I will make my final comments.

It is possible to accept that there may be whole regions of knowledge and experience entirely outside our understanding. What cannot be accepted is that such unknown regions could ever contradict what we already know to be true. We know from a strong body of experimental facts that it is not possible to reverse what is usually referred to as the 'arrow of time'. We know it is not possible to reverse the sense of causality. Yet our experience appeared to contradict causality. An observer on the Earth following our journey would have needed to live for more than a billion years just to cover the first leg of it, the part from the Earth to the quasar. Yet we seem to have arrived back at the Earth at a moment very early in the experience of such an observer, as if on the return from the quasar to Earth we had gone backwards with respect to time. Somewhere, then, what seems to be true cannot be true. Somewhere there has to be an illusion. The question, of course, is where?

With these thoughts in mind I turned to the most mysterious aspect of our experience, that both the ship and ourselves appeared to have been converted to a puff of smoke and yet – yet, here we were, still alive. Could the evaporation have been an illusion? Possibly, but then the first contradiction remained, the causality problem. Perhaps instead, then, the two mysteries were somehow inter-linked. Two mysteries might turn out to resolve each other, like two minus signs making a plus.

It is known that the strongest of all forms of gravitation is the one associated with quasars, the so-called black hole. In the old days it used to be thought that matter falling into a black hole came to an end, it ceased to exist. It is now known that this curious notion is quite wrong. The black hole is compensated by an opposite behaviour – matter emerging in what is called a white hole. My thought in this respect is that our ship, and possibly the Yela too, fell into a black hole and that we emerged again as a white hole. This is clear enough. What is remarkable is the thought that phase relations among all the particles were preserved in such a way that the organizational form of the matter was also maintained in and out of the system. In other words that a ship could fall into a black hole only to emerge *as a ship* from a white hole. Yet in the matter of the laser beam the creature associated with the quasar had shown a total mastery over phase control.

A black hole–white hole situation is a kind of magic tunnel. You go in at one side at some place in the universe and you emerge at some quite different place. Perhaps back again close to the solar system? I wrestled for a long time with this idea, with the idea of the creature at the quasar not only maintaining phase control over our structure but also flicking us back, as it were, to our own home base. The topological setup in a black hole–white hole relationship is known to be exceedingly complex, so at first sight the idea seemed attractive. But then the trouble about causality reasserted itself. I could believe in my 'creature of the quasar', a creature that could do things far beyond human capability, but I could not believe in any creature defying basic physical principles. So the idea of a return to Earth only a few tens of thousands of years into the future beyond my own day was simply untenable. Any return to Earth would have to be some billions of years into the future. Hence I was back squarely with the old contradiction. Even so, I had a feeling of satisfaction in having achieved some measure of conceptual progress.

At this stage I remembered that the universe itself is supposed to possess a kind of black hole–white hole symmetry. To our observed universe there is an inverse universe. The thought struck me like a thunderclap: could it be that we had emerged not in our own universe at all but in the other half, the inverse half? Could it be that the other half had exceedingly similar phase relationships to our half? Given a close enough balance there could be a galaxy like 'ours', a Sun like 'ours' – even a planet with creatures on it like 'ours'. Could we have been guided close to that twin solar system? The causality difficulty might then have conceivably been overcome.

The thought of being guided through a black hole by an intelligent creature boggled my imagination. I was staggered by the three-stage comparison. First, we human beings had managed to move around our planet. We had gone a little way outside even, into the solar system. Betelgeuse and his space people had shown us how to move around the galaxy, but by travelling for very many human generations. The Yela, on the other hand, had been able to move in a few years across the visible region of the universe itself. It had done so without apparent effort. Remarkably, it had done so in a way that we could readily understand. Simply by maintaining an acceleration of a quite ordinary kind, just by maintaining it over a period of several years. But now at a still higher level, the third stage, we had this new creature controlling the properties of a black hole, and doing so in such a way as to maintain communication between entirely different segments of the universe, far outside the range of what could be seen with our telescopes.

At this stage in my deliberations an amusing thought struck me. I wondered what one of the old-time scientific societies would have thought about these ideas. I could imagine the frank expressions of disbelief and derision.

However, once I reached this stage in my thinking I soon established a fact that would have given the greybeards in those societies something to chew on. It was an obvious step to measure the optical rotary properties of living material in the ship. I soon established that it was all dextro-rotatory. Since we had started our travels possessing a levo sense, it was clear that a reversal had taken place. There could be no question but that it had taken place during a brief flash of unconsciousness which followed the moment when the ship appeared to dissolve into a sea of luminescence.

We have been living for some time now on food grown on this planet, which surely means that living material here also has to be dextro-rotatory. Indeed I have verified that this is so. Hence, since living material on the true Earth is basically levo-rotatory, it follows inexorably that this planet, however much it might seem to resemble Earth, is not the true Earth.

I have not told my companions of these thoughts and discoveries. Although we are different varieties of the human species – of the real human species – we are remarkably similar in our psychological makeup. Yet there are some respects in which we are characteristically different. I have lived now with Betelgeuse, Alcyone and Rigel for quite long enough to know exactly where these differences lie. Here, then, is one such difference. I know, essentially for a certainty, that the three of them would become incurably depressed should they be robbed of the long-sustaining hope that *their* people will one day arrive on this planet. It is not necessary to them that such an event should occur in their own lifetimes. So long as they feel themselves to be establishing a planetary port of call, there is meaning in their lives. Rob them of this cultural refuge and their present existence will become utterly empty and bitter.

For myself, the situation is different. In fact exactly the reverse. I feel this inverse universe cannot be precisely the same as our universe. Indeed the dextro-levo difference shows this to be so. I keep wondering if the true Earth really did fail. Was it one of the many planets that reverted to pitiless barbarism? Or was it one of the very few to succeed in breaking through to a higher level? Did the message of the late Beethoven quartets win through at the last? I live in the hope that this was so.

More about Penguins
and Pelicans

Penguinews, which appears every month, contains
details of all the new books issued by Penguins as they
are published. From time to time it is supplemented
by *Penguins in Print*, which is our complete list of
almost 5,000 titles.

A specimen copy of *Penguinews* will be sent to you
free on request. Please write to Dept EP, Penguin
Books Ltd, Harmondsworth, Middlesex, for your
copy.

In the U.S.A.: For a complete list of books available
from Penguins in the United States write to Dept CS,
Penguin Books, 625 Madison Avenue, New York,
New York 10022.

In Canada: For a complete list of books available
from Penguins in Canada write to Penguin Books
Canada Ltd, 2801 John Street, Markham,
Ontario L3R 1B4.